THE ROAD

TO

EZRA

DEDICATION

To my Parabatai, Natasha

I couldn't be an "Adult" without you. Through the highs and lows of life, you've always been there, and I'm so grateful to have you in my corner. Night Tree Pack and Storm Cross Pack, thank you for being the best inspiration I could ever wish for. I also wouldn't be here without all the late-night talks and honest feedback. You've never been afraid to tell me what you genuinely think; your honesty means more than words could ever express. You make me a better writer and a better person. I love you!

To my Loving Husband, Darren

You never gave up on us as I worked through my traumas. You were pivotal in my healing journey. Without your support, I would never have been able to face the demons I had faced my whole life. Although our road has been far from a smooth one, we made it through. You are my Bash. And I only pray to the Gods that I never have to face this world without you. Thank you for loving me.

To my three children

(You better not be reading this until you are adults!), but I love you. And to my Hailey, who was the biggest blessing a broken woman could have ever asked for. Someday, I hope you can understand just how blessed and proud I am of the young woman you've become. Never stop reading, never stop loving, never stop living. Life can be so beautiful. All you have to do is open yourself up to it.

To my dear friend, Brad

You helped me with every aspect of being a writer I didn't realize existed. Thank you for the nights you've spent reading through chapters, offering insights, and all the moments you've spent encouraging me. I hope you know how thankful I am for everything you've done. I hope you make your mark on this world so I can offer you the same encouragement you gave to me.

To my Adoptive parents, Chris, and Mary

You will never know the millions of ways you changed my life. You loved me like I was your own blood, never judged me for my less desirable qualities, and always supported my dreams no matter how crazy they were. You loved me at my worst and at my best. I will always be thankful for you and proud to be your daughter.

To all my Book girlies,

It has been such a pleasure getting to know so many of you. I didn't realize how welcoming the book world could be. I appreciate you more than you will ever know!

SPECIAL THANK YOU TO THE MOST AMAZING ARC TEAM FROM THE BOTTOM OF MY HEART!

Mandi, Alessa, Jaelynn, Summer, Veronica, Natasha, and Sandra, you have been by far the best part of this entire experience. It has been an absolute honor to share my book with you ladies. The love, feedback, and enthusiasm you've shown me made this whole process worth it!

Thank you to my amazing Cover Artist, Muhammad Waqas, who went above and beyond. You are so talented. It's been such a long process, and you've been an absolute dream to work with—you never fail to amaze me! Also, to my Editor, Vicky Anna, you are amazing! Thank you for all of your hard work! This book would not exist without you both. I'm so grateful for all of your hard work!

Note from the Author:

The Ezra rose is a delicate and enchanting variety that blooms in a pale peach hue. As she unfolds, she reveals layers of soft petals, opening beautifully to highlight its graceful form. Every one of you is an Ezra rose. Stay Beautiful, my flowers.

TRIGGER WARNING

This book contains scenes of child abuse, both physical and mental, which can be triggering to some readers. It has elements of BDSM. The FMM experiences thoughts of self-harm. Scenes of hyper-vigilance and narcissism can also be triggering to some readers.

This book contains dub-con, violent scenes, and death. It also contains sexual encounters that explore several kinks, such as knife play, restraints, and edging.

Everything depicted in this book was a product of my imagination and is not meant to be harmful to you or your mental health.

PLAYLIST

NOTHING CAN HURT ME: ERADAZE

NOT OK: MARIA MENA

LUV N RAGE: DANNY ARO, OKAYHANK, MOXAS

DIE TRYING: NEW MEDICINE

FOR REAL THIS TIME: ERADAZE

I BETTER RUN: EREDAZE, MEZSIAH

FMLYHM: SEETHER

I GET OFF: HALESTORM

MAKE U MINE: THEVNKOWN

MIDDLE FINGER: BOHNES

THE KID I USED TO KNOW: ARRESTED YOUTH

K (ALL I GOT TO SAY): NUVILICES, JOSEPH FEINSTEIN

DADDY ISSUES: THE NEIGHBOURHOOD

HOLLOW-LØ'S VERSION: LØ SPIRIT, DABIN, KAI WACHI

CONTENTS

CHAPTER ONE

WHAT WAS THIS GUY, A STALKER?

The distance between my bedroom and the front door was short, but as I tiptoed down the hall, every creak of the floorboards seemed like a whispered warning. The air was thick, almost suffocating, as the faint echoes of my footsteps broke through the unsettling silence. *This was a bad idea.*

The stairs descended into complete darkness. As I placed my hand on the railing, it felt cold and rough beneath my touch. With each step, the shadows grew deeper and more amplified. The feeling of being watched became almost unbearable until I closed the front door behind me, and the chilly night air wrapped me in its chilly embrace. Relief washed over me as I started my 1995 Honda Civic and backed out of the drive.

I hate you, Kit.

As I walked into the party, I could feel tiny flutters in my abdomen. I swallowed the lump forming in my throat before I slipped into the crowd. I tried to weave through the people jumping and swaying with the song's beat, feeling completely out of my element. Everyone was laughing and singing along as Benson Boone's *"Beautiful Things"* came on, blasting through the two large speakers in the frat house's living room.

Being invisible was an art I had mastered, but there were so many people here, and I was already hating myself for coming. Not only were parties not my scene, but I was nervous about sneaking out of the house. I hated giving my dad any ammunition to use against me, but my best friend Kit had been blowing up my phone with texts asking me to come, so here I was.

I scanned the crowd, trying to find Kit and avoiding eye contact with anyone. It was her stupid idea to come here, which wasn't exactly surprising to me. She was a party girl, living her best life. I reached into my purse, retrieving my phone to send her a message.

(I'm here. Now where are you?)

I slid the phone back into my purse and walked to the kitchen, which seemed less inhabited than the other rooms. The occasional grouping of people would come to refill their beers from the tapped kegs on the island countertop. Red solo cups were stacked on both sides of the kegs, and I grabbed one, before heading to the sink.

As I was turning on the faucet to fill it with tap water, I felt my phone buzzing inside the small black purse that sat against my hip. I sat the cup down to pull out my phone, then continued filling it as I clicked on the unread message.

(Boo, with a thumbs-down emoji)

I turned around and sure enough there she was.

"Ezzie, Babes, nobody comes to a party this hot to drink water," she scolded me.

"Yeah, no, I know, it's just that I don't like beer Kit, you know that."

She didn't seem phased by my words. She was already a bit tipsy. She refilled her cup from the keg and lifted it to me, "Well, then I'll just have to drink enough for the both of us!" She clinked her glass to mine.

"That's a horrible idea, Kit."

"Or it's the perfect one because look who just walked in," she pointed to the kitchen door, and I leaned around her to get a better look.

I didn't recognize the man standing there, but he did look like Kit's type. His hair was black and longer in the front. It feathered to the side, begging to have a woman's fingers threaded through it. He wore a black leather jacket over a plain white T-shirt. A single chain necklace hanging around his neck. He was holding his glass in one hand, and the other hand was half tucked into the front pocket of his jeans. He looked like trouble. But admittedly, he was the kind of trouble that pulled you in.

"And that is who, exactly?"

"I don't know," she said, shrugging her shoulders and taking another gulp from her cup, "But he's cute, don't you think? Come on, let's go introduce ourselves."

Before I could protest, she grabbed my hand and pulled me in his direction. *I really, really hate you, Kit.*

"Hey there cute stuff, I'm Kit, and this is my best friend, Ezra," she gladly announced to him. Kit was always like this. Happy and bubbly, and completely unafraid of anything. I think that's what I admire most about her.

"Bash," he replied, but he wasn't looking at her, he was looking past her, straight at me.

I felt a red flush on my cheeks and as my eyes met his, the rest of the world seemed to melt away. The music around us faded along with all the people in the room. The heart beating rapidly in my chest, the only coherent sound. I was okay with being invisible, invisible was safe, but the way he was holding my gaze. That made me feel anything but invisible. My breathing grew shallow, and I took a step back, putting some distance between us.

"Hi." I managed to breathe out as all the noise from the party sprang back to life with a mind-shattering force, causing me to break his gaze. Kit was staring between the two of us, turning her head quickly from his face to mine.

She then hummed, with a huge grin on her face, "Oh man, this is my favorite song! So, I'm going to go dance," She pointed at him and then at me before finishing off with, "You two kids have fun."

"Kit!" I said through clenched teeth, but she was already gone. *This bitch just left me.* He and I just stood there, staring at each other uncomfortably for what seemed like forever. Words were beyond my capabilities at this time.

I watched as he stared at me expectantly. He had raised one eyebrow but said nothing. He was either becoming amused by my inability to initiate conversation, or he was getting annoyed. Either way, I had no intention of sticking around to suffer in this awkward silence for a second longer. Forcing a cringy half-smile as I turned and quickly walked away without a word.

I shot Kit a quick text before searching for an exit.

(What the hell is wrong with you?)

When I found lucky door number six, it led outside onto a small balcony. I leaned over the railing, breathing in the heavy night air now polluting the city and exhaling it deeply, to calm myself. The busyness of the day was evaporating into the night. Although, in the distance, you could see the faintness of red and blue lights.

There were still people walking down the sidewalks, no doubt Oakie's searching for their next great thrill. I could see the silhouette of various tall buildings off the horizon, leaving a bright, glowing hue around them.

The city at night was a sight I would never grow tired of. I pulled my phone back out glancing at the screen before letting out a disgruntled sigh, cursing Kit under my breath.

A loud crash and the sound of breaking glass forced my eyes to the doorway. I was frozen. I stood there staring at the door. After a short pause, I heard hooting and hollering inside, and I felt the sudden tension in my shoulders evading me.

This party was getting crazy, and the only friend I had just ditched me with a random guy, and now I had no idea where she even was. To say I was "irritated" would have been an understatement. I was worried that Kit wouldn't be able to get home safely after drinking so much, which meant I was stuck here until she was ready to go, and she wasn't messaging me back.

I sat down on the patio chair, and leaned my head back, squinting my eyes trying to find the constellations overhead. They were hiding, the city was far too bright to form any recognizable patterns. Though the Moon was big and beautiful, radiating with a force that would never be overshadowed. Oh Goddess, I thought, please let this night be over, soon. I was in complete awe of the moon when I heard a voice behind me asking, "Hey, this seat taken?"

My body jerked, and I turned to face the voice over my shoulder, I couldn't believe it. The guy from earlier was standing in the doorway. What was this guy? A stalker?

"Yes," I said, "I mean no. No, the seat isn't taken, and yes, you can sit if you want to, it's a free country."

He just chuckled as he sat down in the other patio chair, "So, Ezra, right?"

"Hmm?"

"Your name?" he clarified, "It's Ezra?"

"Yes. That's my name," I said, pinching my lips together in a straight line. I was avoiding making eye contact this time. I felt my head bobbing strangely, as another beautiful silence settled in between us, it left me feeling uncomfortable.

I hated silence, as much as I hated noise. In silence, there was so much room for thoughts to wander, which never led me anywhere I wanted to be. As I rose to my feet, he spoke again, "I haven't seen you around before, do you live around here?"

Shit, what if this guy really is a stalker?

I chose not to answer him but instead ask him a question of my own. "Have you seen my friend Kit? The girl I was with earlier?"

"I'm pretty sure I saw her still killing it on the dancefloor, but I can help you look for her if you want," he said as he rose to his feet. Allowing me to appreciate how insanely tall this man was in comparison to my five-foot, three height. He was drawing me in, his whole fit from top to bottom was pleasant to look at, and that terrified me.

I didn't want his help. I didn't even want him here right now. Every interaction between us, up to this point has been steeped in a mix of cringeworthy moments and awkward silences; like a lost melody echoing through the corridors of time.

"I'm good, it's quite beautiful out here when you're alone, one of us should be able to enjoy that," I turned to leave, but then he spoke again, "Maybe I'll see you around, Ezra."

"Or maybe not," I said, "this isn't my scene, but you have fun."

When I got inside, I went over to the designated "Dancing" area, and it didn't take long to find Kit. She was dancing, though not very gracefully, and was still sipping on a beer. "Hey, it's late," I told her, "I'm heading out. I think you've had enough fun, too so let's get you home." I took the cup from her hand and set it on the closest surface I could find, which happened to be the mantle of the large fireplace. She tried to protest me, but I wrapped her arm around my shoulder and started leading her out of the party.

"Heeeeey?" she asked cheerfully, "What happened between youuu and Mr. Cute stuff?" she was slurring her words, and it was painfully obvious, she was not going to remember any of this in the morning, making me laugh.

"Nothing happened, he's not my type, and I'm still mad at you for ditching me like that."

"I wasn't ditching you Ezzie, I was helping youuu," she cooed.

"Yeah, I can see that, but now it's time to go cupid."

The distance between the frat house and where I parked was way longer than I remembered as I pulled her along. I helped her into the passenger seat when we finally got to my car. Once she sat, she cuddled into it, and I handed her a bottle of water and two Tylenol. "Take those," I told her, walking around to the driver's side.

It didn't take long to get to Kit's house. She was two years older than me and was already in college. She lived in a house off campus with two other she-wolves she went to school with. As I pulled in, I honked my horn. The two girls came outside and helped me get her into her bed. I left another water on her nightstand and then thanked her roommates for the help before leaving.

When I got home, all the lights were still out in the house. I turned off my headlights and pulled my car slowly into the driveway. I didn't bother to lock it because I didn't want it to beep.

When I got into the house, I carefully shut the door behind me and twisted the lock. I took two steps towards the stairs before the living room light turned on. My dad was sitting in his chair, the whole living room reeked of beer. And there were empty bottles all over the stands. He stood up and without a word, he began pulling off his belt.

I felt my heart sinking, "Dad, please, I can explain."

CHAPTER TWO

WHAT THE HELL DID YOU DO?

As he folded his belt in half. He made a loud noise like the cracking of a whip, it rang through the air, slicing through the silence. The crack demanded my attention, impossible to ignore, and sent a shiver down my spine.

"You think… that I'm going to listen to anything that whore mouth of yours has to say?"

"Dad, I was just taking Kit home, I swear, there was no guy! I'm sorry," I began but he was already moving closer to me, I backed up until I felt the door pressing firmly against my back. My hands fumbled to find the lock, but I never took my eyes off him. I felt the lock between my fingers so briefly before my dad closed the gap between us.

"I'm not going to have you sullying my good name," he hissed, grabbing me by my hair, my hand falling from the lock, as he began pulling me into his office behind him. He didn't bother using his wolf, he could easily grip me up without it.

"Dad, I wasn't," I pleaded, but he pushed me over the desk, pushing my face down into the mess of documents spread beneath me. It didn't take him long, even against my struggles to rip my skirt off. I was standing there with nothing but my panties on my lower half, exposed in a disgusting way that made my skin crawl.

"You're no daughter of mine," he roared, and then he began swinging his belt.

The first couple of hits burned like a hot iron against my skin, my body was numb by his eighth strike, and I lost count after eleven. Once he grew bored with it, and it was clear it had no more effect on me, he dropped the belt.

"Clean up this fucking mess, Ezra, I trust you can at least do that without fucking it up."

As soon as I knew he was gone, I let myself quietly cry for a moment before I picked up my skirt and made my way up the stairs. I knew it was going to hurt, but I needed a shower, I needed to wash off the blood and filth, so I could bury this moment with all the rest.

I started the shower; it was straight freezing water because I knew it was bound to hurt like hell. Hot water would just intensify the pain. I couldn't see the damage he had done, but I could feel it. As I slid into the shower, the water ran down my back and when it reached my butt, I had to bite into my lip to keep from screaming. It stung all over again.

I watched as the water beneath me was painted red. A swirling vortex of crimson and scarlet, pooled at my feet, like a fiery tornado, as it washed down the drain. Once I could see the water clearing by my feet, I turned off the water and got out. I gently patted my backside with the towel, but that didn't make it hurt any less. Once I was dry, I wrapped the towel around my body tightly and peeked out the door.

The hall was still empty, so I ran on my tippy toes back to my room, shutting the door quickly but quietly behind me. I would clean his office in the morning, for right now I slipped into a large shirt and crawled face down on the bed. Stuffing my head into my pillows, I silently sobbed until finally, sleep took over.

In the morning, my alarm went off, pulling me from my peaceful sleep. As I stirred in bed, sharp, throbbing pains shot up my back and down my backside. A new reminder of why I couldn't wait for my birthday, the pain of last night would soon subside. But until then, I would let it fuel my desire to escape that man. I reached over to my cell phone and looked at the screen.

(Hey Babes! You saved my ass last night, I don't even remember getting home, but I remember Dreamy McDreamy Pants!)

(I need all the details, call me later. Love you.)

I rolled my eyes and put my phone back down. Of course, that's what she remembers. I walked to my closet and pulled out a small ornate box that used to belong to my mother, I kept it stuffed under my stack of sweatshirts. If my dad knew I had this, he'd surely destroy it. Just as he destroyed her and then turned all his anger on me when she had left us.

I pulled out the small bottle of pain pills I had stashed inside and took two before shoving it back in its safe little hiding space, grabbing a long baggy sweatshirt. Pulled on matching baggy sweatpants and made my way downstairs.

Every morning, I started breakfast and brewed Dad's coffee. If I didn't, it would just give him another excuse to hurt me. I had already scrubbed the office clean, and I was finishing up breakfast when he entered.

"Morning Ezra," he greeted me. He would often pretend nothing had happened the night before. He never wanted to admit to the ugly truths of what he had done and who he was. Of course, I knew better than to say anything, that would just piss him off all over again. So instead, I played along. I returned his greeting as I handed him his plate and a steamy cup of coffee.

"Morning Dad."

"Dad, I have work today, did you need anything from the store while I'm out?"

"No, Ezra, I have meetings all day, I won't be home for dinner tonight either, so eat without me."

"Do you know when you'll be home?"

I carefully bent over to put on my shoes as another sharp pain rippled up my back. He never answered me. Which meant this fun, little conversation was now over.

"Good luck with your meetings."

He grunted something under his breath that I couldn't hear, but I wasn't going to ask what. I grabbed my keys and went to work. The day was long and excruciating. By the time I got home, my whole body hurt, from pretending it didn't hurt. I began cleaning up his mess, and once everything was tidied up, I went to my room. I grabbed my phone and saw I had several missed messages from Kit.

(Hey Babes, just checking in!)

(So, Flynn filled me in on McDreamy. you need to explain. He was hot af. Why didn't you talk to him?)

Flynn was one of her roommates. She wasn't in our pack, she belonged to Silver Pack, but she went to the academy with Kit. She was a nice girl; she hated parties as much as I did and had left early. Not early enough though, as she had seen Kit and I talking to Bash. She had asked me about it last night. I answered her questions with a shrug, saying, "I don't know; Kit was pretty tipsy when I got there and thought he was cute."

She just laughed because she knew as well as I did that it was Kit. *No fucks given.* Ever.

(You'll never guess who I just ran into?!?!)

(It was McDreamy! And he was asking about you!)

(Ezzie, he wants to know if he can have your number.

Yes, or no?)

(Ezzie?! Gave him your number! Don't be mad.)

(Love you.)

Kit, what the hell did you do? I closed out of our text chain. She had no idea, the trouble I was already in, and now I have to deal with this Bash guy, on top of that? I went to close out of my messenger app when I saw a notification for a new message with an unknown number. *Oh shit, Oh shit, Oh shit!* I didn't look at it, I just slammed my phone face down on my nightstand. I refused to look at it. My best friend did not just give my number to a potential stalker. It's just spam. It had to be spam. *Fuck me.*

I was sitting there on the edge of my bed staring at my phone when I heard my dad walk in.

"Oh Ezra..." he was calling my name from downstairs. I peeked out of my door and heard his feet crunching on the stairs, but I didn't answer him. I went to the nightstand, grabbed my phone, and tucked it into my sweatpants. Praying for the Goddess, to please not let him be drunk again.

"I know you're here you little, Bitch."

Unanswered prayers weren't uncommon for me. Sometimes I didn't know why I even bothered anymore. I went to my door to shut it, and when he saw me, his mouth curled up into a sadistic smile.

"Found you."

I slammed the door shut and locked it. When he started banging on the door, I jumped back. He had a strong wolf, and I knew it wouldn't keep him out for long. Why did the Goddess hate me?

"You thought I forgot didn't you, about your whoring around," he was slurring his words, as his banging on the door became more powerful, every impact, causing me to flinch back farther from it.

I backed up to my window, sliding it open, and glancing out over the edge, to the cement driveway below. It wasn't going to be a fun drop, I already hurt like hell. It was still probably the better alternative. I climbed through, lowering myself down until I was barely hanging onto the window ledge. I closed my eyes and dropped. I let out a pained cry, the lower half of my body braced for the fall, but when I hit, I fell straight back on my ass.

When I finally got to my feet, I looked up at the window to see Dad's wolf staring down at me. In its fiercest form, eyes glowing with wild hunger. Drool pooled in the corners of his mouth as he snarled down at me from above. Desperate to escape, I turned on my heels and began to run. The howl, primal and fierce, cut through the frigid night air behind me. Making every hair on my body stand on end, urging me to get away before it was too late.

The ground beneath my feet began to blur as I sprinted away. I didn't know where I was going, I just knew my body couldn't manage another beating, so I had to get out of there. I was somewhere in the middle of town before I slowed down to peer over my shoulder. No sign of him. I had sweat dripping from my forehead, but the adrenaline temporarily shielded the pain I had been feeling all day.

A bunch of guys walking down the sidewalk gave me a creepy side-eye. So, I walked into the small diner to my right, and when they didn't follow me in, I sat down at a small booth. I dialed Kit's number, but it just kept going to a dial tone. *Fucking Hell, Kit. Answer your damn phone.* I went to my messages to send her a text. But that "One Unread Message" notification got my attention again. I clicked on it opening the message display.

(Hey Ezra, this is Bash, from the party last night… I know you said parties aren't your scene. Maybe you can show me what your scene is, sometime.)

This is so stupid Ezra. You don't even know him. But I was desperate. I hit the call button. It only rang a few times before I heard a voice on the other end, "Hello? Bash's Banging hotline," said the voice.

"I'm sorry, I think I have the wrong number," I was saying just as I heard another voice. "Damnit, Zayne, give me my damn phone." And then he spoke into the phone, "Hello? Ezra?"

"Hey, Bash. You said you want to hang out."

Oh, Goddess, help me.

"Yeah, I do. When do you want to meet up?"

I took a deep breath; it was too late to take it back. "Can you pick me up now?"

CHAPTER THREE

GOOD GIRL

"Now, as in right now?"

"It's okay if you can't, I would understand if you can't just drop everything and come get me."

I didn't want to tell him what was going on. This secret is one I've kept since my mother left us when I was eight years old. I already felt stupid calling him in the first place, but now I was wishing I had used even the tiniest bit of my brain to just delete that message. There is no way he'd come get me now, just because I called him. I mean, that's *crazy.*

"Where are you? Can you drop a pin?"

"Yeah, one sec."

I put him on speakerphone as I sent him a pin to my location, inviting this absolute stranger to my exact location. I was still confused as to why he would drop everything for someone he barely knew. *Really, who is this guy?*

"Got it. I'll see you soon," he said before hanging up the phone.

I didn't know what I looked like, and to be honest, I didn't care. I wasn't trying to impress this guy. I was convinced he wasn't even my type. I know that dark, mysterious, and handsome was just asking for an entire world of hurt, and I had enough of that in my life already.

Plus, if there ever was a guy. I would hate to see the way my dad would react when he found out. I just needed to get away from here, and Kit wasn't answering her phone leaving me with no choice.

Still, I went into the bathroom, pulled my hair up into a loose ponytail, and splashed chilly water on my face, to wash away the sweat that I had gained running here. It was about 10 minutes before my phone buzzed again in my pocket.

(I'm outside.)

I pushed my hands into the pockets of my grey sweatpants and made my way outside. Bash was leaning up against a large black motorcycle. It looked like a type of sports bike; he had his helmet in his hand pressed up against his side and a mischievous grin on his face, confirming my initial prediction. This guy was Trouble with a capital "T." Who knew his smile would take the air right out of my lungs, though? I mean, you've got to be kidding me. This guy somehow managed to become even sexier at that moment.

"Hey, you ready?"

"Um, what is that?" I asked, nudging in the direction of his motorcycle.

"This?" he asked, holding up the helmet, "It's a helmet, Ez. To protect that pretty little head of yours." He mused to himself as he made a knocking gesture on the top of it.

"Yeah, I can see that." I said with an eye roll, "I just mean, you don't expect me to get on that death machine, do you?"

"It's not a death machine."

"Are you insane?"

I looked from him to the motorcycle in shock, but he just chuckled. He let his hand glide down across the curves of the bike. He was either admiring it or speaking some language I didn't yet understand. Because it sure as fuck wasn't answering my question.

"Come on, Ezra. Live a little."

He started walking over to me, helmet in his hands, before holding it out for me to take. I took my signature deep breath before accepting it from him. But then I was just staring at it in my hands, like an idiot.

"I don't know how to put this on," I said, looking up at him.

His tongue moved over his bottom lip before sucking it between his teeth, a sexy grin spreading across his features before he shook his head at me. Apparently, this was amusing to him. He took the helmet back, sliding it down over my head. I truly didn't want to do this, but it was better than staying here. He tilted my head up with his finger, then began tightening the strap against my chin.

"How's that feel?" he asked, releasing the straps.

"Good."

He then tucked the loose straps in before sliding the cover down over my eyes, and I followed him to the bike. He swung his leg over and kicked the stand up, pulling the bike into an upright position. He started it up, and the engine roared. He then patted the seat behind him.

"Just put your foot on the peg, and swing your leg over," he explained, and I nodded. My body was still hurting badly, but I managed to swing my leg up and over.

"Good girl," he said before turning to me, "Now hold on to me."

I just sat there, looking for anywhere else for my hands to go, then on him. He didn't like that. "Put them here," he said, grabbing my arms and wrapping them around his torso. I didn't say anything, as he pressed them firmly onto his body. I could feel his sturdy frame beneath my touch, and it was exhilarating. He patted my hand, reassuringly.

"Just keep your body in line with me, when I lean, lean with me, if at any time you want to stop, just give me a pat, and I'll stop okay?"

There was something so calming about the way he spoke to me, and something about the way he said, "Good girl," that made me stop fighting his actions or words completely. I could feel all the tension in my shoulders floating away the more he moved his mouth. I became hyper-fixated by the way his lips were moving, the small dimple that formed next to them as he spoke.

"Hang on tight, Ezra."

When I squeezed my hands together firmly, he smiled again, pulling off the side of the road. The bike sped up insanely fast. My body jerked back, causing me to tighten my grip on him. He didn't seem to mind, instead, he reached down with his left hand and began rubbing my arm until he was going at a steady speed.

The more he drove, the more relaxed I was beginning to feel. The wind was wafting around us in a cool, satisfying way. Slowly my grip loosened around his waist. Eventually, I felt so at ease that I released my grip completely. I slowly put my hands out to the side, allowing them to dance in the wind, winding up and down like they were surfing through the air, as the buildings and people came and went in a blur.

I was laughing now, this felt so freeing. I closed my eyes and allowed myself to get lost in that feeling. His hand on my inner thigh pulled me back to reality, he was rubbing little circles on the inside of my thigh, causing my body to heat up in an unfamiliar way. I wrapped my arms back around his hardened stomach muscles, and as if that were his cue, the bike sped up.

We drove like this for a long time before he pulled off and into a gas station. When he pulled up to the pump, he shut off the bike. And tapped my leg, I knew he wanted me to get off, and I complied. He set the bike down on the stand as he too, swung his leg up over the bike, letting it lean into the kickstand.

Then he popped the shield that was covering my eyes up. He was smiling, a deep, charming smile that spread through his features and up to his eyes. His hair was more fluffed and flowing than when I met him last time, no doubt from the wind, but it didn't look bad. It made him look even more attractive.

"Thanks," I said as I began fumbling with the straps on the helmet. He pulled me closer to him and with little effort, un-did the tie, and helped me pull the helmet off.

"You did good, one could even say, you were having fun," he said as he reached up to "Boop" my nose, causing my nose to scrunch into my face. And then he was laughing at the face I made. Causing a pure and naïve desire in my heart.

"I'm going to go pay for the pump, Come with me?"

I nodded in agreement, and he placed the helmet on the bike, then held out his hand for me to take. I hesitated, I was looking at his welcoming hand in front of mine, and part of me wanted to take it. The other parts of me though, knew that was a terrible idea. I decided to listen to my head, instead; smacking his hand like I was giving him a high five and moving past him towards the gas station.

That might have been even more embarrassing than if I had just taken his damn hand. Sometimes I question how I was ever going to function in society. Other than Kit, I never talked to anyone. I barely left my house, except to go to work. Or the occasional outing with Kit.

Soon he was beside me and we walked the distance to the gas station in silence. When we got there, he rushed in front of me, opening the door for me to enter. He kept surprising me. Seems he's dark, mysterious, handsome, dependable, and a gentleman, too.

This list of his just keeps growing, and I found myself wondering if I did want to get to know him better.

"Are you hungry? We could get some dinner if you want to, I know this beautiful place close to here, Best Pancakes ever."

"No, I'm okay," I laughed, but my stomach let out a small growl.

"Snacks it is then," he said grabbing a variety of goodies and throwing them up on the counter. The cashier gave him a *"What the fuck*" kind of look, but he seemed unfazed, "Can you go get us some drinks?"

"Sure, what do you want?" I asked, turning, to go towards the rows of coolers that lined up the walls.

"Water, baby girl."

My cheeks flushed, and I quickly turned away from him. Hoping he didn't see. I grabbed two bottles of water and returned to the counter. After he paid, we went outside and walked over to the side of the building.

"Be right back."

I watched as he headed back to the pump where we left his bike. His nice little ass caught my attention as he walked away from me. Even the way he walked was sexy.

Goddess, quit playing with me.

CHAPTER FOUR

FRIEND ZONE

--Bash's POV

After I filled the tank, I rode my bike over to a side parking space next to where she was waiting for me. I could still feel her lingering touch on my abdomen. And my wolf, Kane, was reveling in it. I could tell she was anxious at the beginning, and I was trying to soothe her, the little touches I stole on that ride were fleeting and did nothing to fulfill the lustful longing of my wolf.

Kane had never perked up like this before. Something about this awkward, yet beautiful creature just drew us both to her. I wanted to have a real conversation with her, so I bought a few snacks and some drinks. When I got off my bike, I sat on the curb, but she continued to stand.

"You know, I won't bite," I joked as I patted the ground next to me.

"I'm fine standing," she replied, there was something else, but she didn't say it. I looked at her for a moment, before accepting that she wasn't in the mood to share, "Alright. So why don't we go for a walk?" I asked as I stood up patting the dirt off my jeans.

"Sure," she laughed, and I held out my hand to her again, hoping she would take it this time. Last time, she rejected my touch, high-fiving me like we were buddies, instead. But this time, she accepted my hand and allowed me to thread my fingers into hers as we walked. I loved the way her hand felt in mine. Her tiny fingers threaded with mine, ignited something within me that was spreading like wildfire. Electric shivers ran down my spine, fueling a desire that was burning hotter with every moment.

"So, you go to the academy with Kit?"

For once, she was initiating a conversation with me. And I couldn't help but smile.

"Yeah, I'm ending my junior year, how about you?"

"Oh, I don't go to the academy."

I already knew that, because I had searched her name in the school database after the party. I know that was very creepy, but this girl genuinely intrigued me. She either didn't know who I was or just didn't care.

Right now, only one Ezra currently attended the school, and it wasn't this cute little redhead before me. That was how I found her friend Kit. Who I had managed to coerce into giving me Ezra's phone number. That took more effort than I would have thought, too.

"Why is that?"

She sighed and then turned to me, "Because I'm only seventeen, I'll be a freshman in the fall."

Her words stunned me. She was only seventeen.

"What were you doing at a college party, if you're only seventeen?"

"Kit made me go," she shrugged, "She's always dragging me into crazy situations, and somebody needs to take care of her, as she struggles to do that for herself."

"Kit's a sophomore, right?"

"Yeah, she'll be a junior next year, and she seems to think you are pretty cute," she laughed. I liked the sound of her laughing. But I was struggling to wrap my head around this now.

"What do you think?"

Right now, her opinion was the only one I seemed to care about. I couldn't figure her out and it was messing up my head.

"I think you're exactly her type."

"That's great, but I'm not interested in Kit."

I felt this intense pull towards her, and Kane seemed to have taken an interest in her, too. She could be my future mate, but she wouldn't feel any of that until she turned eighteen and received her wolf. I was studying her face to see if she had an interest in me too, but she was still and the growing silence was enveloping us both, making me feel uneasy.

As the wind blew, it felt like time itself had paused. The world around us seemed to fade away, leaving just the two of us in that heavy silence. As I watched her in that silence her eyes, misted over, told stories of memories I couldn't see, but could almost feel.

She was completely disconnected from this place where just moments ago, everything felt at peace. It was like she was lost in another time, another place, and I was just a bystander to her journey. The moment was filled with a mix of peace and unease, like standing on the edge of a dream and reality.

Ezra let herself disappear in that moment for so long, that it startled me when she finally shook it away from her mind. She sighed, a single tear escaping those baby blues, forming a wet stream down her cheek.

"Look, Bash. We don't need to do this." She spoke as she pulled her hand away, and I reluctantly let her fingers slip out of mine.

"Do what?"

I wasn't even sure what we were doing.

Something about her was simply different than most girls. I felt drawn to her, and I had yet to learn the cause. I was also acutely aware of the warmth fading from my hand, as the cool wind blew, drying the sweat that had been forming between our touch.

She said she was seventeen, but she seemed so much more mature than that. This girl had layers, and I wanted to peel them away one by one. I wanted to look into that memory with her and rewrite it in a way that undoes all the pain she was now feeling.

"This," she said gesturing between the two of us,

"The whole, getting to know each other, and making small talk, thing. I'm not the girl you bring home to your parents, I'm just a girl who you're better off staying away from. It will be much easier for us both if you don't push it. I mean, you're what? Twenty? I'm seventeen, I don't even have my wolf yet."

Yup, like I said. This girl has layers.

"Look," she began again, "thank you for the ride, but I think it's best if we just went our separate ways from here."

Wait, what? No way in hell is that happening.

"Ezra, we are more than an hour away from town. Let me get you somewhere safe. And… this doesn't have to be anything more than…" I felt an ache in my chest as I said the next words, "We could always just be friends."

I was looking down at her. She pulled her bottom lip into her mouth, biting down on it, lost in thought. She then reached out her hand to me, "So, friends?"

I ran my hand through my hair, before chuckling and meeting her handshake, "yeah, friends."

--Ezra's POV

Just as soon as he shook my hand, I felt my phone buzzing in my pocket. I quickly released his hand and answered the phone, stepping away from Bash for a bit of privacy. I glanced in his direction, and when I found his eyes on me, a warm smile formed on his face.

"Hey, Kit."

"Ezzie, are you okay? I went to your house, and your dad answered. He said you weren't home, but he was drunk, I could tell."

"I'm okay Kit, I climbed out the window." I was keeping my voice hushed so Bash wouldn't hear what I was saying.

"Well, where are you? I'll come pick you up."

I loved this girl like she was my sister. As much as I protected her, she also protected me. Her family used to live next door to us when I was younger, and she was always so kind. I don't know if her family knew what was going on with me and my dad. If they knew, they never spoke about it.

My dad was one of the elder wolves. He was highly respected in the community, but he was good at putting on a show in front of others. I'm sure to most he seemed like a kind, loving father. Behind closed doors, not so much. Whenever I couldn't be at home, they would let me stay with them. Kit became my safe space, and I owed her for all the pain her friendship had shielded me from.

"Actually," I paused, thinking of how to phrase my next words. I trusted her with everything, but I didn't want her to make a big deal out of this.

"I'm with a friend, but can I meet you at your house?"

"Of course! You know you are always welcome here, Ezzie. Love you, Babes! See you soon."

"See you soon," I said before hanging up the call and returning to Bash.

"Think you could take me to Kit's house?"

"Sure," he said, but the smile on his face didn't seem genuine, it almost seemed forced. As we walked back to his bike. We picked up all the snacks that were scattered about, and he handed me his helmet, which I happily placed on my head.

This time I wasn't afraid of getting on his motorcycle, I was excited. I remembered the way he had been so calm to me, as he rubbed my arm, and rubbed little circles on my thighs causing all my fear and anxiety to wash away.

He reached up, tightening the strap for me once again, and jumped on the bike. He backed it out of the parking space and then motioned to me with the swing of his arm, it was my turn, and I quickly got on. As soon as I placed my hands on his abdominal muscles, he took off. The ride to Kit's house seemed long, I hadn't realized we had gone so far away from town, but I was thankful to him for this experience.

When he pulled up to the house, he shut off the bike and helped me out of my head armor. Strapping it to the back of his bike. Then he pulled me into his embrace. I didn't know what to do, it had completely taken me off guard.

I just stood there, frozen in place, with my hands at my side. Imagine a penguin, that's what I looked like. *A fucking penguin* and I'm sure the whole event looked as awkward as it felt. It was at least brief. When he realized I wasn't returning the embrace, he released me and his hand shot up, ruffling his hair as he chuckled nervously.

"Sorry, I figured it was okay to hug a friend goodbye."

I couldn't form a single word; I gave him a half-smile before turning and maybe? Running to Kit's house. I don't remember the walk from him to where I was currently standing in front of her door. But I was glad when I turned the knob, and the door opened freely. I couldn't look in his direction. That was completely humiliating. I shut the door and made my way to Kit's room.

CHAPTER FIVE

WHO DOESN'T LOVE SOME GOOD GOSSIP?

I knocked on the door to Kit's room and it instantly flew open, revealing a face I couldn't wait to see.

"Ezzie, details. Now."

"I'm sure I don't know what you mean," I said shaking my head at her, but when I stepped into the room, I saw Flynn and Beth. They were staring at me like I was keeping some mind-altering secret, which caused my brow to rise as I turned back to Kit. Whatever was going on here, was sure to be a nightmare for me.

"You know exactly what I mean!"

"Kit, it's been a long day, I'm going to need you to use your big girl words now, because I swear to you, I have no idea what you're talking about!"

I was already beginning to put the pieces together. Either Flynn or Beth saw that humiliating event outside, and while I was trying to pretend it never happened, it did. And these girls were not going to settle until they heard all about it in detail. But still, I was hoping that I was wrong.

Confrontation.

Just thinking the word, made my heart race. It was the very same reason why I tried to avoid parties, or anything involving large crowds of people. But right now, I was being cornered by three girls, which was terrifying.

"You said you were with a friend!?"

"I was with a friend, Kit." I said hugging her, "And now I'm with my best friend!"

"You didn't tell me your "friend" was Bash Bingham!"

"Why are you yelling at me, Kit? You're the one who gave him my number, remember?"

I had no idea what was happening right now, but Flynn and Beth were so invested that Beth fell off the bed from leaning in so far to hear all the juicy details.

"Shit, sorry, continue. Pretend I'm not even here," she said, sitting back down on the bed, which just made us all bust out laughing. After we all caught our breath, Flynn broke the silence, "Kit..." she urged.

"What is the big deal?"

"Okay, you have to promise not to be mad," Kit was taking my hand and leading me to the bed, prompting me to sit down.

"Okay, Kit. I'm listening, now will somebody please tell me what is going on?"

"You were just with Bash Bingham," said Beth.

"Okay?" I was still utterly confused.

"He's Alpha John's son," Flynn continued for her.

"WHAT?!" I rose to my feet, "No, that can't be right."

"Oh, but it is," said Beth, "That was Bash Bingham, as in the new Alpha of Night Tree Pack. I saw him outside on his motorcycle, and I also saw… well actually I'm not sure what I saw, what even was that?"

She was talking incredibly fast, and my mind went back to that awkward hugging interaction between Bash and me. *Oh shit!* Forget leaving my dad's home, after this, I should probably leave this time zone. I was pacing around the room, and mumbling under my breath, when I realized the silence was suddenly deafening, in a room with four girls. I turned to the bed, and they were all looking at me.

"What?"

They all looked at each other and then Beth broke the silence, "Well, what were you two doing together? How do you even know him? It makes no sense."

"Yeah, inquiring minds want to know," Flynn pitched in.

I huffed out an exasperated sigh, before sitting back down. I was not getting out of this conversation without spilling the tea. And while I enjoy I nice warm cup of tea, I wasn't in the business of giving it out. Unless I was at work, in which case, yeah. That's exactly what I did.

"Come on, Ezzie," Kit was smiling again as she rocked back and forth with her knees cradled to her chest, "He's the Alpha heir, and who doesn't love some good gossip?"

"It isn't even what you think, I tried to call you Kit, but when you didn't answer, I called Bash."

"Wait? Does he know about what happened?" she asked suddenly, she didn't say it out loud with the other girls here, but I knew what she was talking about.

"No, he had texted me earlier asking if I wanted to hang out, so I took him up on the offer, that's all."

"Still doesn't make any sense to me, why would our Alpha be interested in a little girl." Beth piped in.

Kit shot her a look. One of her signature, "Fuck around and find out" looks, which shut Beth up.

"I have no idea, Beth. We barely talked at the party, but he still wanted to hang out."

"And he showed up on a motorcycle!" Flynn cooed, "How sexy can he be? The difference between our Alpha's is insane!"

"Yes, he showed up with a motorcycle. I hated the idea of getting on there with him but… "

"But he's a super hunk, and you couldn't help but be swept away by his charms…" Flynn cut me off.

We all laughed again, except Beth, who shot Flynn a dirty look.

"No." I corrected her, "Do you want to hear the story or not?" I asked the girls, getting annoyed by their constant butting in of the story.

"Yes, sorry, our lips are sealed," Kit said, pretending to zip her mouth shut, then she nudged the other two who followed her lead.

"It wasn't like it was a date or anything, I didn't even want to go with him, but he can be very convincing. So, I agreed, and we went for a ride. We ended up talking for a bit when we stopped to get gas, he said he wanted to be friends, and then he brought me here." I finished.

I left out all the other details because it seemed like a personal moment between him and me, and it honestly meant nothing. So, it wasn't any of their business. I also didn't mention that awkward hug, because well, it was humiliating.

"That's it?" asked Beth, standing up off the bed, "Then what was with that hug, thing I saw outside?"

"He hugged me goodbye, which caught me off-guard."

"Yeah, it didn't seem all that affectionate, come to think of it. So? You two are just friends?"

"Yeah, we are only friends," I assured all the girls in the room.

After Beth and Flynn realized I wasn't going to be giving out any other details, they left the room, leaving me and Kit alone, which was great. Because honestly, I was exhausted. Every part of me, mentally, physically, and emotionally was drained. I was ready to curl up with my bestie and get a few hours of much-needed rest.

As soon as they were gone, Kit leaned up and said, "There's more, right?" as she was wiggling her eyebrows at me.

And again, we were laughing, but this time she didn't pressure me for details, she reached up and pulled me into a warm hug. I crawled up next to her in bed, and she was brushing her fingers through my hair, as she would often do when I was younger.

"Ezzie? How bad did he hurt you?" she asked just as I was starting to fall asleep.

I didn't want to give her the answer, but I knew she cared for me like a sister as well, and she hated it when I was in pain. It would hurt her more if I didn't tell her, so I opted for option C.

A tiny mistruth.

"Not bad, Kit." I felt sleep pulling me in when I heard her whisper, "Liar." in my ear.

"Yeah," I whispered back, "I know."

I stayed with Kit for a few days, after that first night. I was afraid of facing my dad. But I didn't have any clothes here, and Kit, while I love her, had an entirely different fit and build than me. She had seen what Dad did to me, and she didn't want me to go back.

The idea was weighing heavily on my mind, but in truth, I was worried he would come looking for me, and whatever horrible situation it would bring with it, it wouldn't be only my burden anymore. So, for Kit's sake, I had to go back.

Bash had messaged me every day while I was at Kit's, but I didn't respond to them. I figured, soon enough, he would forget about me. I had learned from Beth and Flynn that he had every eligible she-wolf at the academy vying to be his future Luna. So, new-found friendship or not, that was a whole other headache I didn't want or need right now.

It didn't stop me from thinking about him. I don't know why but I kept replaying the feeling in my mind, of him rubbing tiny circles on my thigh. The calming caress of his hand on my arm, as he assured me, I was safe. No one had ever touched me like that before, and as insignificant as it was, it was calming to me, and it inhabited a small space in my mind.

When I got home, I stood outside on the front porch, trying to force myself to open the door. I sat on the porch swing that was never used and searched for any inner strength I could find. When I did go inside, my dad was sleeping in his usual chair. Or he had passed out, I couldn't tell the difference anymore. The house was a mess, he hadn't picked up anything while I was gone. I began picking up the empty bottles and putting them in the recycling bin. When I got closer to him, he stirred in his seat.

I decided it wasn't worth waking him, so I left the bottles around him and went upstairs to my room. My door was broken and barely hanging on the hinges, something I would have to fix eventually. I grabbed some clothes to get changed and went to the bathroom, I was in the shower when I heard my dad's voice on the other side of the door.

"Ezra? You're back?" he asked.

"Yeah, Dad. I'm back. I have work soon though, so I won't be here long. I didn't mean to wake you," I said turning off the water and wrapping my towel tightly around my body. I opened the door, and my dad was standing there.

Dad looked relieved to see me, which made me feel bad for being gone for so long. "There's an event in town next weekend at the main packhouse, think you can get off of work?"

"Yeah, I can try," I answered, just as he pulled me into a hug. He didn't say sorry, he didn't say anything at all. It was one of those rare moments when he was just my dad. I couldn't even remember the last time he hugged me, but I hugged him back.

"I love you, Dad." I said as he stepped back, releasing me from his embrace. He didn't say it back, he didn't say anything, he just turned and went back down the stairs.

The next few weeks were uneventful. Kit and I went shopping for the perfect dresses. Her and her family were going to be there, too. I ended up buying a simple silky green dress, that cut off mid-thigh. It hugged my curves, complimented my figure, and had a halter-top. I paired it with simple diamond earrings, a diamond bracelet, and silver heels.

When I descended the stairs, my dad was waiting in one of his black suits, he was checking the time on his watch and looking annoyed that it took me so long to get ready. When he saw me, he opened the front door, and I grabbed my purse before walking to the car waiting out front.

The ride was mostly silent, when we got there, dad cleared his throat before saying, "You look beautiful, Ezra."

I couldn't stop the smile that spread across my face, "Thanks Dad, so what is this for anyway?"

"Alpha John is hosting the event for his son. It's his 21st birthday, so he'll be taking over as Alpha. This is his accension to the throne," he said as he exited the car and reached his hand down for me to take. He helped me out of the car, and we walked the long stairs leading up to the packhouse, as we walked my dad said, "He hasn't taken a Luna yet, so I'd like you to spend some time with him."

I wasn't expecting this, but suddenly everything was making sense. He wanted me to help elevate his station. That was what this whole night was about, and he had no idea that I had already met

Bash, or that I had already set boundaries with him. We were just friends.

CHAPTER SIX

YOUR SECRET IS SAFE WITH ME

--Bash's POV

I looked out the window, staring down at the Night Tree Pack members who were currently flooding the gates. The rise of a new Alpha was a huge moment for our pack, and all the key players were here to witness it. As my father's son, this was my responsibility. I have been training to take over the pack my whole life, but that didn't loosen the tie around my neck. I ripped it off, tossing it to the side, and unbuttoning the top button of my shirt.

"Your dad isn't going to like that," Zayne said walking in.

"Yeah well, unfortunately for him, I'm now in charge," I said as I picked up the suit jacket, tossing it on and ruffling my hair.

"It's your funeral, but don't worry bro I got you; I'll speak the truth at your funeral. Here lies Alpha Bash, his reign was short, almost as short as his..."

"Shut up, Zayne." I cut him off.

"Dude, we all know why you bought that motorcycle," he laughed, cracking himself up.

"Oh, he got jokes," I said, as I punched him in his shoulder and then took off running down the hall towards the pack dining room. When he finally caught up to me, he was breathing heavily, "Bro, did you get faster?" he asked.

"He's got jokes, but no stamina, bet the girls love that" I laughed.

"I've had zero complaints," he said proudly.

I patted him on the shoulder, as I pushed the door open. People were already gathering at the tables. The dining hall was massive, it seated about two hundred people, so it was a great place to host pack parties and events. It was always open to anyone in the pack, although usually only the pack Gamma who resided here, the staff, and my family used it.

As I made my way to the main door, several pack members stopped me saying congratulations and introducing themselves and their families. I knew a lot of the men, and I went to school with most of the girls. I had no interest in getting to know any of them, but I had messed around with quite a few. Never anything serious, most of them just lacked personality or depth.

I greeted them all politely and thanked them before excusing myself, so I could repeat the process again with all the other members. When I made it to the main door, my mom and dad were already there greeting each pack member as they entered. My dad looked at me and shook his head before grumbling something under his breath. It had been 30 minutes of this, "Hi, Welcome. Thank you, I appreciate it. Have a fun time," nonsense before I looked up and saw a face, I hadn't seen in weeks.

Ezra.

She was walking in, on the arm of an older gentleman. I had seen him around plenty of times with my dad, but I didn't know he had a daughter.

"Eldor Thorin, we're so happy you could join us," my mother greeted him.

Then my dad reached out his hand to him, "Hey there, Thorin. It's good to see you, man."

The man reached out shaking his hand in return.

"Ezra, my you have grown." My father said, turning his attention to her. She was blushing as she greeted him in return, "Thank you, Alpha."

Eldor Thorin then turned to me, reaching out to shake my hand, "Congratulations young man, I hear you have a very bright future ahead of you, I'm looking forward to collaborating with you," he said shaking my hand.

I returned the gesture, "Thank you, sir. I only hope I can lead our pack as well as my father here."

"He's been a great Alpha, indeed," he agreed before moving Ezra closer to me, "May I introduce my daughter, Ezra? She'll be turning eighteen soon and is set to attend the academy next fall."

I looked at Ezra, who was trying hard to hold back a laugh, "It's very nice to meet you, Alpha."

I grabbed her hand and lifted it to my lips, placing a small kiss on the top of it, "I hope we can talk later, Ezra."

"That'll be fine, fine indeed," her father said before moving forward into the crowd, pulling her behind him.

Most of the night came and went in a blur. I spent most of it, trying to find my way to Ezra, only to be stopped in my tracks by another man, introducing me to his daughter. A few times I managed to catch a glimpse of her watching and laughing quietly to herself. She was enjoying my misery. And I was going to make her pay for that later. Finally, I gave up. I pulled out my phone.

(You are enjoying this)

(You aren't having the time of your life? lol)

(Oh, so you are seeing my messages?)

(I've been busy.)

(When can I see you, again?)

(Idk, there's a pretty extensive line, could be a while)

(Let's get out of here, meet me outside in five?)

(...okay.)

--Ezra's POV

When I got outside, he was sitting out front on his bike. He had lost the suit jacket. I bent down and undid the straps on my heels. Picked them up and ran down the stairs to meet him. When I got to the bottom, Alpha John came barging through the packhouse doors.

"Sebastian!! Get your ass back here!"

Bash looked at his dad and then back to me, "Now or never, Ez."

I quickly kicked my leg over and squeezed him tightly. Only our second ride together and I was already a pro. I turned and watched as the packhouse disappeared into the distance. I threw my hands up over my head, screaming out in delight as we hauled ass out of there.

When we got to the bridge overlooking the Monongahela River, he pulled off to the side of the road. We got off the bike and I leaned over the railing.

"This is so crazy, I can't believe you left your party!"

"I wouldn't have had to, if you would have talked to me," his voice was serious, but I chose to ignore that.

"And miss out on watching you speed date the entire pack?"

"You are asking for trouble, Ez. It's not funny," he picked up one of my curls, twirling it around his finger, "I seriously feel like I'm being pimped out to the pack."

"Yeah, that sucks."

He chuckled, "Your words are so helpful, Ez. Truly remarkable."

"Always here to help," I laughed, "But I do have a serious question for you."

"Hit me," he was looking at me now.

"You need to explain, Sebastian?"

"You caught that did you?" he raised an eyebrow at me, "Bash is a nickname, my full name is Sebastian Elias Bingham, but when I was little, I had a lisp, I couldn't say it. I was sick of people making fun of me, so I started telling everyone my name was Bash."

"No way, I don't believe it, "the" Bash Bingham, has a lisp?"

"Had," he corrected, "but if you tell anyone that, I will deny it."

"Don't worry, your secret is safe with me," I said pretending to lock my mouth and then throw the key into the river below.

I spent the rest of the night with Bash. I had texted my dad to let him know I was staying at Kit's house. I knew that was a lie. And if he called Kit, she would also know that was a lie. But she would cover for me, so I wasn't very worried about it.

Bash and I drove all around the city that night until we found ourselves outside of city limits. I had never been outside of Oakland before and I loved how all the buildings seemed to disappear until it was just Bash, Me, and the open road. The air smelt differently too. It had this freshness to it, that made everything feel light.

It seems so silly now, how I used to be afraid of his motorcycle. Cause being with him, riding around, his body between my thighs, his abs beneath my fingertips, his hand on my knee, nothing in this world could ever begin to compare to that feeling. I was high on the thrill of it. When he finally pulled over for gas, I couldn't feel my ass. It was numb, from the humming of the bike, beneath it. I swung my leg over and jumped off.

"How are you doing? That was a long ride, you feeling okay?"

"Other than, not being able to feel my ass I'm perfect."

"Would you like me to feel it for you, baby girl?"

His tone was playful, and it surprised and excited me. I let him pull me in closer to him, as he helped me remove my helmet. Then before he could "Boop" my nose, I got his. His head shook in confusion before reaching down and tickling my sides. I wiggled between his legs trying to escape, fighting for my breath. My heartbeat thumping in my chest. I was begging for him to stop, through forced words, my lungs hated me for speaking, but then his arms were around my waist, and I almost thought he was going to kiss me.

It would have been the perfect first kiss. But we were just friends. After a minute he let me go. When he went to pay for gas, he smacked my ass. I gave him a shocked look, and he just smiled.

"You didn't say, no."

I sat on his Zoom Zoom, imagining how free it would feel to be so much more than a glorified backpack. I made a mental note: Someday, I will have one of my own.

Someday when I was, finally, free.

After that night, Bash and I would spend time together when I had time. I spent the entire summer working as many shifts as possible at the café. I needed the money for when I started school in the fall. I also wanted to save for a sexy little Kawasaki Ninja ZX-6R, I had found. Bash said I shouldn't start on a six hundred CC motorcycle. He thought it might be too powerful for me to start, but I didn't care.

That bike was my ticket to freedom, and I wanted it more than I think I have ever wanted anything in my entire life.

Summer seemed to go by so fast.

I was excited to begin classes, I was packing all my things when Dad walked in.

"Instead of moving on campus, why don't you just stay here?"

"I told you, Dad. I want the whole experience. I need to be out on my own."

He turned, going back downstairs, not pushing any further. *That was weird.* I was only in the shower for a few minutes before I heard my dad's voice outside the bathroom door.

"Your mother tried to leave me, and now you think you're going to leave me?"

"Dad? Can we talk after I get out?"

"I'm done talking."

Fuck.

I didn't even have time to turn off the water, I grabbed my long T-shirt and somehow managed to pull it over my head before he flung the shower door open. He used so much force that the glass shattered, and I jumped back against the shower wall, screaming. My body folded in on itself and I slid down the wall, cradling my legs in my hands.

"You aren't leaving me!"

"Dad, I'm not leaving you, I'm just going to college!"

I lied.

"You're no better than your mother!"

He was grabbing me by my leg and pulling me out of the shower before I had time to react. My head smashed against the wet shower floor, as tiny pieces of glass tore through my back.

"Dad, please stop, I'm not leaving you, I'm here, I'm sorry, I'll stay!"

I knew that pleading with him did nothing but fuel his desire, but I couldn't stop the words from coming out. He dragged me into the hall, and I managed to land a kick to his stomach, knocking him back away from me. I hauled ass to my bedroom but remembered a minute too late that he had broken down my door last time, and I hadn't fixed it yet.

I ran to the window, but it wouldn't open. *That fucker screwed it shut.* I picked up the closest thing I could find and punched it through the window. But it was already too late.

I braced myself for the impact, as his fists began striking me repeatedly. He was telling me how worthless I was, how nobody would miss me if I were gone, how I was nothing but a whore like my mother… as the pain intensified, a small part of me hoped I wouldn't wake up from this. This was way worse than his usual beatings. This was the worst pain I'd ever felt. At that point, I wished I were dead, anything to stop the pain.

I don't remember the rest of what happened, but I woke up several hours later, in a bloodied mess on the floor. I crawled to my phone which was now lying under my bed. It was a pure chance, that it was at a level I could reach, there was no way I'd be able to get up to it, where it usually sat on my nightstand.

It must have been knocked off the stand during the events, which left me crippled on the floor. I went to my messages, but I knew I couldn't message Kit, I needed her to be safe from this. I texted the only other contact on my phone. Bash.

(I NEED YOU.)

CHAPTER SEVEN

PARALYZED.

--Bash's POV

I pulled out my phone to text her again when Zayne yanked it out of my hand.

"Come on, Man. What the hell, give me my phone back!"

"No way, man. You cannot keep messaging this girl," he opened my desk drawer and threw the phone in, before slamming it shut, "If she wanted you, she'd have texted you back by now. At this point, it's looking a bit desperate."

"I am not desperate, Zayne. There are hundreds of girls hitting me up daily."

"Exactly, so why the fuck are we chilling in our dorm room? We should be out there," his hand swung out towards the door, pointing like there was some magic world on the other side of that door and not a long empty hallway lined with boys' dorms.

"You go," I said before opening the drawer, grabbing my phone back out.

I put it in my pocket and threw my hands up as if I were surrendering, "Don't worry, I won't message her again."

Summer was over, and the next school year was beginning. Zayne and I had just finished moving into our dorm suite for our senior year at the academy. We could've moved into a house off campus, as we usually did, but I knew Ezra would be living in the dorms, so I chose to stay here too. Zayne, being my Beta, was stuck moving in with me.

Over the summer, we spent time together a handful of times after the party. Ezra worked a lot, and sometimes she wouldn't respond to me for weeks at a time. I hated not being able to spend time with her, but every day with her was a new adventure and worth waiting for; to say I liked her was an understatement. Anything I could do to be closer to her was worth it.

Zayne sat on the couch and grabbed the PS5 controller, then looking at me he said, "Best three of five?"

"Yeah, why not," I said, "Though it seems pointless, as we both know I'm going to PWN your ass."

"Keep dreaming, bro," he laughed.

We were in our fifth match; the score was 2-2 when my phone buzzed in my pocket. I paused the game and pulled it out. When I saw her name, I couldn't help but smile. She finally texted me back. When I opened the message, it simply read (I NEED YOU). I jumped up and grabbed my leather coat and my bike keys.

"Come on, man, it's our last game," Zayne was whining, but I didn't care, she needed me, and I was going to find her. I opened the door and left without a word or backward glance.

I was already on my bike and driving towards the city center when I realized there was one major flaw with my plan. It wasn't like I was thinking with my head. The impulse was driven by something, well much lower. All her text said was, I NEED YOU.

What the fuck does that even mean? She needed me, how? I wasn't exactly sure what situation I was preparing to walk into. Part of me, well okay, most of me wanted her to need me in the most vulnerable way possible, preferably without clothes. But she only wanted to be friends, so what did she need, my help moving into her dorm? I mean, friends do that, right?

During our almost-date, last year, we had agreed to be friends. I hated that. But I wasn't exactly able to argue. I agreed to be friends, just because I couldn't have her, didn't mean I couldn't keep her close.

Nope, wrong. She completely ghosted me, often. So, was she in trouble? I tried texting her back a few times on my way to the garage to grab my bike, but she never answered.

I don't know what type of witchery she was up to, but she had completely enveloped my thoughts. The more she pulled away from me, the closer I wanted to be to her, especially because my wolf seemed drawn to her too, always perking up when she was close. Not that any of this mattered, because the one major flaw in my current plan to be there for her, was that I have no fucking clue where I was going.

I had asked her once, the night we met, if she lived around here. Instead of answering my question, she blew me off. When we did spend time together, it was never at her house, and she would usually just meet me somewhere. I'm beginning to think that secrets might just be her thing. Something I never experienced before. Sure, she was incredible to look at, but it wasn't in my nature to chase a woman. They usually just threw themselves at me, and I found it frustrating that I didn't have that effect on her.

I did know where Kit lived, and she would hang out with us sometimes over the summer, I would even consider her a friend. I hit the throttle, shifted into sixth gear, and disappeared into the distance. I was banking on her knowing where I could find Ezra. When I pulled up to Kit's house, there were still lights on, so I knew someone was awake. I was hoping it was Kit.

The door opened, and there was a girl I had never seen at the door.

"Hey, I was wondering if Kit was home?" I said to the girl, who just stood there staring at me. I didn't have time to deal with a fangirl. Usually, I would be patient while they worked through the shock, but Ezra Needed me and right now nothing else mattered.

Before even thinking, I pushed the door open, "Excuse me," I said, quickly brushing past her. When I got inside, I didn't know where I was going so I just yelled for Kit, who then exited the room to my left.

"Bash?"

"Hey Kit, I need Ezra's address," I explained to her, but she was just staring at me now too. *Fuck, do any of these girls know how to speak?*

"Kit, I need it now."

"Well," she began, "I don't think she would want me to tell you, I'm sorry Bash, but I'm sure she'll text you when she's ready." This little she-wolf was irritating me. Doesn't she get it? I need to find her.

My voice was growing louder now, "Kit! She did text me, and now she isn't answering me, she needs me," I watched as she lifted her hand to her mouth, the color was now draining from her face.

I held my phone out for her to take, "The address, Kit." It was no longer a question, and she nodded, grabbing my phone and plugging an address into Google Maps, "Go," she said handing me back my phone, "I'll be right behind you."

When I got to Ezra's house, the door was wide open. I ran in, and everything was trashed. I began checking every room, looking for her. At the top of the stairs was the bathroom. Walking in, all I could see was blood and shattered glass everywhere, and I felt a tightness in my chest, making it hard for me to breathe.

Fear had crept in, stopping me in my tracks as my eyes scanned the room, taking in every detail. *She was in here…this was her blood.* I took a deep breath, sending a silent prayer up to the Goddess that she was okay.

My wolf kept whimpering. He was noticeably quiet until now, but I'm sure he sensed my panic intensifying. When I got to the end bedroom, the door was smashed through. I walked in and there she was.

Her body was so still, I felt paralyzed.

Every curve of her body told a story of what happened there, but I don't think even my darkest mental pictures could touch this reality. She had cuts and bruises lining the lower curve of her ass, which was completely exposed. She was wearing nothing but a large T-shirt that was pulled up, clinging to the dried blood staining her body, only reaching her middle back. The rest of her was completely naked. I saw several long cuts across her ass, which were partially healed, and I had to fight back the tears. *Ezra, what happened to you?*

I rushed to her but feared touching her, I didn't want to ever cause this girl physical pain. But right now, I didn't know if she was even alive. So, I gently pulled the shirt back down to cover her body, slowly turning her over into my lap, cradling her like she was a small child. Hoping that somehow, my closeness could bring her comfort.

"Ezra? Hey, I need you to wake up now, baby girl," I said as I leaned down to check if she was breathing. I felt the faint whisper of her breath against my ear. It was still warm and hot. I had to pull back, as I breathed in her intoxicating scent. I was fighting the urge to nuzzle my cheek to hers, when I felt my wolf coming forward, **"Mate,"** he said as I stood, lifting her easily in my arms.

"Kane?"

"Save her Bash," he whined, **"Save our mate."**

I walked quickly and carefully out to my bike. I swung my leg over and climbed on, still cradling her in my arms, I let her head press into my chest as I started my bike and rode like hell towards the hospital. Car horns blared, as I weaved in and out of traffic, leaving her red, flowing locks, sashaying in the wind, like a flame in the night, illuminating the world with its fierce beauty. A testament to the wonder of who she was. MINE.

As I entered the hospital, this beautiful creature in my arms, several doctors rushed over to me.

"What happened? Can you tell us her name? Give her here son, we need to get her on the bed."

I knew that I needed to let go of her, but I just couldn't. I pulled her into my chest, holding on for dear life. She was mine, and I wouldn't let anyone take her away from me.

"Son, let her go. Focus. Can you tell us what the girls name is?"

Several doctors and nurses were here now, trying to pry my mate from my arms. When the large male doctor grabbed ahold of me, a feral growl ripped from my throat as I snapped canines in his direction.

"Don't fucking touch me!" I snarled, laying her gently on the bed. I began to rub my hand down the sides of her face, leaning over my barely breathing mate.

"My Ezra, it's gonna be okay, baby girl. You're gonna be okay," I whispered, trying to convince myself as much as her. Then, several doctors and security personnel burst into the small makeshift room of the ER, pulling me away.

"You need to let us do our job! Get this guy out of here." One of the doctors shouted, and then I was being dragged out of the room, away from the only thing in this world that mattered to me anymore.

I watched her unmoving body as the doctors began touching her everywhere, trying to assess her injuries, and anger rose to the surface, bringing Kane with it.

"Collapsed lung," said one of the nurses as I fought to get back to her.

"Prep the OR, and somebody get this guy to the lobby!" shouted the doctor again.

CHAPTER EIGHT

INEVITABLE LIES AND MISTRUTHS.

--Ezra's POV

As my eyes began to blink open, scrunching to shield themselves from the brightness around me, the cloudy images began to clear. I reached up to my eyes to rub the fog away, but I felt something pinching in my arm. I groaned, everything still hurt. The clearer my vision became, the more pain I could feel. I quickly decided against that motion, letting my arm fall back to my side.

Just then, a nurse entered the room, drawing my eyes to the door, and the two police officers on the other side of the window.

"Hey there, you gave us all quite a fright," she said shooting me a wide smile, "you are a very lucky, girl."

I raised my brows at that, she thinks I'm lucky. Is that some kind of cruel joke? I sure as fuck did not feel lucky. I would even wager, I ranked high on the ladder of unlucky.

"Can you tell me your pain level on a scale of 0-10 with 0 being no pain and 10 being a tremendous amount of pain?"

She walked around the bed and began fidgeting with the machines next to me. As my gaze followed her, they fell on the man lying in the chair beside the bed. He was sitting with his face cradled in the nook of his elbow, which was propped up on the armrest of the chair. And then my mind flashed to the last moment I remembered; I had texted him before passing out.

"He's been here the whole time," the nurse was looking at me endearingly, "he must care for you deeply. When he brought you in, it took most of our staff to hold him back, so we could get you into surgery. He didn't want to leave your side."

My lack of conversation must have worried her, cause then she put her hand over mine. "Can you tell me your name?"

"Ezra Ken," I answered.

"Ezra, you're safe here. Don't worry, we've already called Eldor Thorin to let him know you're here. I'm sure your father will be so relieved to hear you're awake now and doing well. I'll call him when we are done here, but for now, can you tell me your pain level?" she asked a second time.

When she spoke my father's name, everything else seemed to fade away, leaving me searching for answers in my mind, that I would never find. And it was mind-numbing.

"I don't feel anything," I said after a while.

"Oh, that's great, the meds are doing their job, then!" she said moving back to the door. "I'll be back to check on you shortly, you should get some rest, you've been through quite the ordeal." Before she exited the room, she looked out at the officers standing outside the door, "Since you're awake now, these officers would like to ask you a few questions, would that be, okay?"

"She will not be answering any questions right now, I already told the officers they would be able to speak to her, once she's healed." Bash's voice broke in, and the nurse just nodded in understanding and left. Then he was leaning forward so that he was closer to the bed and looking at me, threading his fingers in mine, "I'm so happy you're awake," he said, "How do you feel?"

His touch always brought me comfort. But when he threaded his fingers into mine, it wasn't comfort I felt. It was pain, deep in my core. I pulled my hand away and was staring at it, as I flipped it over. I don't know what I was looking for, but that strange sensation felt alien to me.

"How long have I been here?" I asked him.

He pulled his hand away and ruffled it through his hair in the same awkward way he often did.

"Two days," he answered, adjusting himself in the chair so that he was sitting back against it, as if he knew I needed more space between us right now. Two days? That meant that I had missed registration for the dorms at the academy. Now I needed to either find an apartment or move in with Kit.

"Well, I should probably say thank you for not letting me die on my birthday,"

When I said it, he just looked at me in complete shock before asking the question that was now heavily weighing on my mind as well.

"Do you feel your wolf?"

"No," I didn't feel my wolf, I should probably be upset about that, but I wasn't surprised.

"Those officers are going to want answers," he said, pausing as if he was trying to find his words. "You don't need to talk to them until you're ready, Ez. I can't even imagine what happened to you, or what you're feeling now."

"I don't…" I started to say before stopping myself. Honestly, I didn't even know what to say. The truth was so ugly, a secret I had kept close to me, guarded, for the last ten years of my life. It wasn't that I didn't want to trust him, I couldn't. The night I met him, I never expected to see him again, but he kept showing up for me. I knew how to be alone. I knew how to suffer in silence. I didn't know what to say or do now. He had seen me at my worst. Broken and beaten down until there was nothing left, but the flesh and bone that held me together.

I didn't want to feel anything for him, right now, I didn't want to feel anything. I was scared to show him who I was. I didn't want him to see the scars on my body or know about the ones in my heart. Maybe he would run away, just like my mother had. Leaving me once again, to break alone in silence. Or worse, maybe he would stay.

What if he tried to help me, but I was too broken to be fixed? Like a porcelain doll that had been pushed off a shelf, splintering into a hundred tiny pieces. No matter how hard you try, that's a puzzle no one could ever piece back together. This mess? My life? I would never ask him to be a part of it.

"You can always talk to me," he said, moving closer, gently cradling my cheek in his hand. I felt that shocking feeling again, this time though, my heart was fluttering as well. I leaned into his touch. I closed my eyes, allowing his touch to soothe my soul. Then I felt his lips on mine.

I wasn't sure how to respond to that, my eyes flew open, this sudden shift in our dynamics had me panicking, and I felt a sudden urge to escape it all. Feeling cornered, in both this situation and this bed. I pushed him away from me and started pulling at the IVs and chords attached to me, trying desperately to free myself from their grasp.

"Ezra? Stop, what are you doing?" Bash asked confused by my reaction.

"I'm leaving," I said, as he reached down grabbing my hands trying to get me to stop. He was saying something, but I couldn't hear the words. The more I struggled against him and all the things that kept me in place, the deeper my hysteria became. All I could hear was my heart beating ravenously in my chest.

"Ezra, STOP!" his voice echoed just as he pulled me into his embrace, with tear-filled eyes.

"Friends don't kiss friends," I shouted at him, "Just leave me alone!" It would be easier for him if he just walked away. I couldn't let him into my life, not in that way.

"I can't do that Ezra," he said, voice cracking, but refusing to loosen his embrace.

"I don't want you here!" I yelled at him; I felt his body tense up at my words before several nurses and doctors rushed into the room. Then they were pulling him away from me, and pushing me down into the bed, holding me down as I continued fighting for my freedom.

"NOOOOO, don't touch me! Get OFF me," I was screaming as they sedated me.

Soon, my body was blissfully numb, and as my eyes betrayed me, falling shut, I felt sleep enveloping me. The only sound was the faint beeping of the heart monitor, as it all faded away around me.

A few hours later, I woke up again. This time, cuffs were securing my arms to the bed, and Bash was gone. Kit now sat in the chair he was once in.

"Hey Babes, how are you feeling?" she asked.

"Kit," I smiled, "I'm glad you're here."

"Ezzie, I'm so sorry, I shouldn't have let you go back. I didn't think Thorin would ever hurt you like this. You need to tell them the truth, about everything, you nearly died this time, if Bash hadn't found you…"

"Hey now, I'm okay." I cut her off, I didn't want to have any conversation involving Bash.

"Why didn't you call me?" she was crying now.

"Kit, if I had called you, you would've come, and you could be lying in a bed next to me."

"You aren't going back there," she said with finality.

"Apparently, I'm not going anywhere," I said, nudging my head in the direction of the cuffs. I was trying to make light of the situation, not for my sake, but for her.

It worked. She chuckled and then began explaining something about how they thought it was best for me, as I was a danger to myself. We both knew the only danger to me was my dad. I'm sure we were both thinking it, but neither of us said it. We sat there and talked for a while before that nurse from before walked in, "Ezra, the police still need to speak with you." I looked over to Kit, giving her a reassuring smile.

"I'll come back and check on you in a bit, then, unless you want me to stay?" she asked as she gave me a big hug.

"It's okay, Kit. Why don't you go get some food? I'll still be here when you get back." I gave her a big smile and wiggled my wrists in the restraints. "Promise."

She let out a loud snorted laugh at that, she knew I was hinting at my joke from earlier. Then she left the room. I swear this girl just got me like nobody else ever would, but even she didn't know everything.

I waited and waited for the officers to enter. I knew Kit wanted me to unburden myself and tell them it was my dad, but she didn't understand why I didn't want to do that. It wasn't about protecting his secrets; it was about saving me from my own. I had a decade of suppressed memories and terrifying events I had no intention of reliving. So, I was writing every plausible explanation for what had happened to me. Rehearsing in my mind the inevitable lies that would soon escape them.

I was deep in thought, weighing my two options, neither of which I liked when I heard a knock on the door. Two officers entered. Greeting me with friendly smiles. Their nametags read, Carter and Chase, on their uniforms. They started asking me basic questions at first, like my name, my age, and where I lived.

As soon as that wrapped up, my dad barged into the room, startling both men. He rushed over to me, giving me a big hug. I couldn't return his embrace, and I found myself suddenly enjoying these cuffs on my wrists.

"Oh Ezra, I've been worried sick. When I got home the house was trashed and you were missing," he began, "Thank the GODDESS," he exaggerated her name, "that you're okay."

Both Carter and Chase took a step back and then the one called Carter said, "We'll give you a moment with your daughter Elder Thorin."

Damn, his acting skills were on point today. I almost believed his words until the officers left, and he narrowed his eyes on me.

"What did you tell them, Ezra?"

I gave him an unamused shrug, "Nothing."

"You know I didn't mean any of that, I had a few too many drinks that's all. You will tell them that it was a burglary and then I'll allow you to return home."

I couldn't hold back the scoff that slipped out after hearing his words. I knew he couldn't touch me, not here, not in the hospital with police officers posted outside my door. He usually didn't talk about what he did. He was above reproach. The only time I had ever asked him why he would do what he did, and why he didn't love me, was forever burned into my soul.

Him, kicking my feet out from under me. The sinister smile that followed, spreading across his face, was imprinted in my mind. As I struggled to get to my knees, hugging my arms tightly around my stomach, where he had just punched the air out of my lungs. His eyes were dark and cold and bore into mine, there was so much hate behind those brown eyes as he slapped me and spit on my face.

"Because you need to know your worth." He had said.

His words had haunted me for so long. Lingering there in the darkest corners of my mind. They would often resurface, and every word, each syllable, carried a weight that pressed heavily on my heart. It was true though; the only person who would even realize I was gone would be Kit. I was worthless, and it didn't matter how hard I tried to change. The more that I did, attempting to appease his temper, the worse it would be when I faltered.

It didn't take long before I found myself overthinking every move I made. I wouldn't speak, afraid of saying the wrong thing. I wouldn't cry, worried it would irritate him. I wouldn't leave the house; to avoid accusations of sleeping around. I was exactly what he wanted me to be, a broken empty shell of a person. My only hope since I was eight was getting my wolf and burying everything, including him in my past. I had been counting the days until I turned eighteen.

I am eighteen now and the present I got from my dad was a new memory to haunt me. The very memory that landed me in this hospital bed, nearly ending my life.

"Being a drunk isn't a good enough excuse anymore, Dad." I spat his name at him.

I saw anger flash in his eyes, before he said, "You look so much like her, your mother, it's disgusting. I can hardly stand the sight of you most days."

"So, you want me dead because I look like my mom? Noted." Of all the excuses he's ever given me, this one cut the deepest.

"If I wanted you dead, Ezra, you would be," he countered.

"How can anyone be so cruel?" I asked him, with sad eyes. I'm sure if I had any tears left to cry, they would be pouring out at this point, but there were none.

"I've taken care of you ever since that bitch left us, you should be thanking me for everything I've done for you."

"Oh, that's rich, coming from the man who has used me as a punching bag ever since she left, someone who would strip me to my underwear and then…"

"Watch your tongue," He was pissed now and he cut me off.

"Don't worry, I won't tell them your secrets, but when I get out of here, I don't ever want to see your face again!" My voice was hushed so no one would hear them, but it was forceful. He said nothing as he turned and walked to the door, opening it, and allowing the officers to return. I guess since he was getting what he wanted, there was nothing else to talk about.

He stood there lovingly as I gave them my statement, "I don't remember much, I was in the shower when the bathroom door flew open, some guy dressed in all black and wearing a mask smashed the shower door open and yanked me out, the last thing I remember was hitting my head. It must have been a burglary."

They seemed to accept that response, and it didn't take long before they were leaving. My father shook hands and the three of them had decided to investigate this burglary, to see if they could find a lead. They wouldn't, because they were chasing their tales, but if it got this man out of my life. I could live with that mistruth.

"Don't worry, Elder Thorin, we'll find the guy who did this to your daughter," the one named Carter said before leaving.

"Keep me updated on the investigation," my father said in return. He waited for a few minutes until he was sure they had left, then he turned and walked out of the room. When he was gone, too. I was completely and utterly alone.

This time, the tears found me as if everything from this day came to surface. Somehow, I managed to push Bash away, when all I really wanted was for him to stay. Then I lost my dad, too. Something I had been waiting for my whole life, but it didn't make the reality of it hurt any less.

My body was trembling, and I could no longer hold them back. My restrained wrists made it impossible to wipe them away, so the tears ran freely down my cheeks. How can anyone be so *worthless* that both their mom and dad would leave them?

CHAPTER NINE

YOU'VE FUCKING RUINED ME!

"Uuugh, Ezzie! It's been weeks, you can't avoid your life forever!" Kit pleaded; she had been trying to get me to go with her tonight, for well over 30 minutes.

"I'm not trying to avoid my life, Kit," I answered, annoyed with her now, wanting this conversation to end. For the first time, I felt like I could finally stop holding my breath. I wanted to live my life, I just wanted to do it far away from every campus party. That way, there was no chance of running into Bash. I felt freed from the ghosts of my past, but filling that void now were new demons.

I had been trying so hard, not to get attached to Bash. But somehow, I still had feelings for him. The moment he challenged me to admit them though, I pushed him away. Or more so, I started acting like a complete psychopath and I couldn't bring myself to face him.

"Is it because of Bash?" she asked, staring at me knowingly.

"Yes Kit, I can't okay, I just can't see him," I answered her with my own pleading eyes.

"Look. Beth said he isn't even going to be there, so why don't you come with me? You haven't even left the apartment except to go to work and I think you could use some fun with your bestie!"

"How does Beth know what Bash is or isn't doing? That's a little cringe."

"They grew up together, her dad used to be our Beta," Her answer made me less tense, if they were friends, that made sense, and I was happy I wouldn't have to face him.

"Fine, I'll go," I told her, and her face instantly lit up.

"You know what this means, right?" she asked.

Warranting an eye roll, I asked, "What Kit, what does this mean?" However, I wasn't sure I wanted the answer knowing who I was talking to.

"This means, we need to go shopping for the best outfits! You need something sexy, so you can find a new man and forget about "He Who Shall Not Be Named"." She was showing her inner geek, and it was a good look on her.

"A Harry Potter quote? Really?" I asked laughing. She just shrugged her shoulders and then we got ready to go shopping. I was certain the whole point of this day, wasn't to find me something sexy to wear to the party, but more for her to dress me up like a real-life Barbie doll.

I tried my best not to complain, because this made her happy, which made me happy, too. By the end of our day, I had successfully bought a new outfit for the party. I went with a cute pair of low-rise jeans with an accented belt and a cross-strap black crop top that left my stomach exposed. I didn't love that, but Kit had talked me into it saying I had amazing abs, and I needed to show them off, and that it made my boobs look good. I tailored it with a cute denim jean jacket.

She bought a bunch of new outfits too, and then we stopped to get lunch. The café we went to was called The Porch. It was a nice café close to campus and featured a large window that was beautiful and offered a magnificent view. We sat and ate, chit-chatting about when we should arrive at the party.

"Okay, so we can't show up too late or everyone will already be drunk, and not too early, cause then we will look like idiots," Kit was explaining.

"So, when do you want to go then?" I asked, just to keep the conversation flowing, I didn't care either way. I was half-listening to her, but I found my eyes wandering, scanning everything around us, until they landed on the small TV against the back wall, the news was playing, and when I saw my dad's face on the screen, I stood up walking over to it.

The two officers from the hospital, Carter, and Chase, were with him and they were talking about how they had a lead in the case involving the string of burglaries in our area.

Kit had followed me over and I turned to her and in a hushed voice said, "There were no burglaries other than the one I had lied about. What lead could they have?" She was at a loss for words, which was completely out of character for her. I turned back to the TV and saw them post the picture of a guy who was a bit older, "Suspect is in his late twenties to early thirties, if you have any information please call your local police station," Officer Carter said. Then the man's picture kept flashing on the screen.

We grabbed our stuff, paid the bill, and headed back to the apartment to get ready. I couldn't get that news broadcast out of my head, though.

Did my dad just frame an innocent man, to cover his ass?

I hated this. Who knew one lie could cause so much damage?

It was about 9:15 when we got to the party. I was surprised it wasn't a frat house party. Instead, it was at a big hotel. This wasn't my first college party, but usually the ones Kit dragged me to, were in different frat or fraternity houses. As I looked around the space before me, I felt excited. String lights hung all over the outside courtyard, casting a gentle, warm glow that illuminated the space beneath them. There was a fireplace in the center, which people were all sitting around.

There was a guy playing guitar and singing by the fire, and I found myself gravitating in that direction. His voice was nice, and as I got closer, I saw him take notice of me. Then he sang the chorus like he was serenading me alone, never looking away from me as he strummed the chords singing, "You're my melody, my sweetest tune. With you, my heart sings under the moon. Every day, every night, I'll be by your side. In this love song, forever we'll ride."

It was beautiful, and I felt a warmth rising to my cheeks. Once he finished, he set the guitar down thanking everyone for the applause, as they cheered for him. "Wow, he is a hunk," said Kit beside me.

I looked away from him, back to Kit. She had a big smile on her face.

"I don't know," I said, suddenly feeling extremely awkward with so much exposed skin.

"Well, you might not seem to know, but seems like he does," she said as she pointed behind me. I peeked where she was now pointing and saw the guy who had just been singing, he was walking towards us. I turned back to Kit, narrowing my eyes back at her, "Don't you dare ditch me." I demanded.

"I have no idea what you're talking about," she laughed.

"Kit, I mean it."

"Sure, fine, I will stay and be your third wheel," she said, and I accepted that answer.

"Hey, Kit!" he greeted her. Wait. What? Did she know him?

"Gabe." She said flashing him one of her big mischievous smiles, "Looking handsome as ever, I see. And with your very own posse."

He brushed that off with a flick of his hair, "Thank you, you look great, too."

"Well, duh," she said. I was starting to feel like the third wheel, when he turned to me and said, "Who is your beautiful friend, Kit?"

I didn't say anything, as I watched him take notice of my very revealing outfit.

"This," she said, pausing to grab my hand and pull me in next to her, "is Ezra, my bestie." She finished. That made me chuckle, and I looked up at him as he grabbed my hand, lifting it to his face, and placing a kiss on the top of it before saying, "Well Ezra, you are without question, the most breath-taking woman in this whole party, and It's great to meet you."

"That song was beautiful," I said, and he smiled, flicking his hair to the side again.

"Thank you, when I wrote it, I was imagining my dream girl, but I never thought she'd walk into my party, how lucky am I?" he asked.

"Wait, this is your party?" I asked and he smiled again. It was a nice smile, but suddenly Bash's smile flashed in my head. The way he smiled, left me breathless, and nobody would ever be able to match that. Not even this super good-looking man in front of me, I felt a pain in my heart, as I thought again of Bash.

"Yeah, it's not a big deal, my parents own this chain of hotels," he said simply.

"I mean, it is kind of a big deal, you are also Silver Pack's new Alpha," said Kit. She looked at me, "But should we go get some drinks?"

"Sure," I said, then I smiled at Gabe, "It was nice to meet you, Alpha," I said as Kit pulled me away, leaving him standing there smiling as we disappeared into a sea of people.

Once we got inside the hotel, we found our way to the open bar. Kit got ahold of the bartender with a smile and a flick of her hand. He quickly came over to serve her. She was stunning, and it wasn't uncommon for men to fawn over her. She exuded a confidence that I would kill for.

"What can I get you two lovely ladies?" said the bartender.

"Something as hot as you, what would you suggest?" she flirted.

"One Hot Toddy," he answered, "And for you?" he asked, turning to me.

"She doesn't drink," Kit responded to him for me. He looked at me curiously and asked if I wanted a mocktail. I agreed with a kind smile. Then he shot a wink at me and turned to make our drinks.

"Girl, I am so proud of you! It's like a baby bird taking flight, you had an actual conversation with Gabe."

"Yeah, so what is the deal with him? You know him?" I asked.

"Oh babe, not that well," she laughed, "I've never really hung out with him, but he's a pretty popular guy at school, with his whole hot and brooding musician vibe."

"His voice was fucking sexy." I blurted out.

"Yeah well, he seemed to notice your sexy lil' ass too!"

"Kinda hard not to, when half my body is hanging out," I said gesturing to my outfit.

"Girl, you are hot and spicy all on your own, with or without these clothes."

"Agreed," the bartender chimed in, "Your drinks ladies." He handed Kit her drink and then handed me mine, with a napkin. When I looked at it, it had his name and number on it. I looked back up and he was down the bar, but his mouth curled up in a flirty boyish grin when he saw me looking for him. Which made me blush again. Is this what it's like for her? Not hiding herself away and just being seen.

"One drink won't hurt," I said waving him back over.

"Missed me already?"

I asked him to get me something else, which he seemed happy about. "I get off in about an hour, can I find you then?" he asked.

"You are welcome to try," I said pulling Kit behind me as I walked out of the bar. As soon as we got back outside, she stopped dead in her tracks and was staring at me with her mouth gaped open.

"What?"

"Are you kidding me? What was that? I mean who even are you? Girl, that boy was putty in your hands…I didn't know you had it in you."

I was sipping on the cocktail the hot bartender had given me, and I was feeling pretty carefree. This was the same feeling I had, whenever I was with Bash. He crept into my mind briefly, but I pushed him out of my head and began dancing. Swaying my hips from side to side, rolling my body, dipping my ass down and back up again slowly. The more I danced, and the more I drank, the more fun I seemed to have, but I was hot. I lost my jacket at some point throughout the night, and when I saw Gabe, I was tipsy.

"Hey, looks like someone is having a good time," he said as I approached him.

"Actually, yes. I am."

As he pulled me down into his lap, I wrapped my arms around his neck, looking down at him flirtatiously. He let out a deep, throaty growl, as I felt his dick growing in length beneath my ass. Then he whispered in my ear, "Do you have any idea what you're doing to me?"

"Oh, shit. I'm sorry," I said beginning to stand but he pulled me back down to his lap. He was breathing heavily as he ran his fingers down my stomach. "I don't..." I began, but then he stopped, at my pant line. The softness in his touch caused a shiver to run through my body.

"Don't worry, nothing will be happening tonight, you've had too much to drink. And when I get you, I want you all to myself."

He started tracing circles around my belly button, and my head leaned back instinctively, as goosebumps formed beneath his touch. He tangled his other hand into my hair and gently pulled my head back, kissing up the nape of my neck. A needy moan escaped my lips, and he let go of my hair, giving me back control over my head. And then I was breathing heavily, too.

I thought he was about to kiss me, and I was debating kissing him back. When I heard a familiar voice behind me.

"Ezra?"

My breath caught in my throat as I stood up from Gabe's lap and turned towards him.

"Bash...what are you? I mean, I thought you wouldn't be here." My tone was questioning and accusatory with a hint of embarrassment.

Had he seen all of that?

"Clearly," he said, but as his eyes fell over my appearance, he seemed hurt. I folded my arms over my stomach in an attempt to hide all the exposed skin. "Do you like him?" he asked, looking from me to Gabe. *How was I supposed to answer that? Was I even supposed to?* I had only just met this guy. Gabe stood up and put his arm around my waist, pulling my attention back to him.

"Sorry Bash, no disrespect, but she's mine."

In an instant, all that hurt evaporated into a fuming rage that radiated from Bash as he narrowed his eyes on Gabe. He stepped forward, pulling me from his arms, landing a hard right hook to Gabe's jaw that knocked him to the ground. Simultaneously, lifting me over his shoulder. He carried me, kicking and screaming, out of the party, pulling everyone's attention to us.

"Bash? What the FUCK! PUT ME DOWN," I screamed as he walked me out of the party, everyone had been watching, and I was so far past embarrassed. I was fucking pissed. He didn't say anything, he just kept walking until we reached his bike, he set me down on it, pushing his helmet into my hands, "Put it on."

"No! Bash you can't just…"

"Ezra, I'm not asking." He cut me off, as he reached up rubbing his temple. "Just put it on, for once would you stop fighting me and just do what I'm asking you to do? Put on the damn helmet so I can take you home."

I slid off the bike, setting his helmet down on the seat, and looked at him. "Bash, you can't just make decisions for me. I was doing fine in there, and I can find my own ride home."

"Damnit, Ez. Don't you see he was never going to take you home? Don't be so naïve," He was gesturing wildly with his hands as he spoke, "He had his hands all over you, Ez," he was pissed, but the faint quivering in his voice betrayed him.

"You can't just punch every guy that touches me!"

"The fuck, I can't. I'd burn this whole town to the ground before anyone lays another finger on you."

"Bash! Would you just listen to me?" I let out an exasperated breath, rolling my eyes.

"No," he said simply, before picking me back up. He grabbed the helmet from the seat and sat me sideways on it. He was pressing his body between my thighs to steady me from falling, and then he raised the helmet over my head. Before he could put on my head armor, I reached up, cupping his face in my hands, forcing him to look at me.

"Bash…I can't be everything you want me to be," I wasn't yelling anymore; my voice was calm and steady as I told him, "We've been down this road already, Bash; I'm not the girl."

"Fuck Ez. Don't you get it?" He said, giving up and hanging the helmet over the handlebars, "You're the only one I want; you've fucking ruined me." Then he leaned down over me, bracing his weight on his hands, which were now on either side of me. Leaving me pinned between his hard body and the leather seat of the bike. He was so close, and I could almost taste the sweetness of his hot breath as he continued.

"I want all of you, every insufferable part, 'cause when you're not around, driving me crazy, everything is just harder. I don't want to be your friend, and I won't let you go…Ez, I can't." Then his hands were around my waist, pulling me into him, as he closed the final distance between his lips and mine. They were soft and hot against mine and I let myself evaporate into the heat of that kiss.

An intense wave of warmth spread from my lips to my core, radiating outward, igniting my skin as my heart began beating more rapidly. I pushed deeper into the kiss, wrapping my legs around his body, which fit perfectly between them. I felt my cheeks growing flush as this all-consuming warmth spread through my veins, growing more intense with each passing second.

I had never felt more alive than, at this moment. And like an addict, it felt like fire burning me from the inside out, when he pulled away. I wanted more, so much more of him. We were both breathing heavily, when suddenly that intense fire began searing my skin. I was crying now, I looked up at Bash with tear-filled eyes, "What's happening to me? It hurts, so bad."

He pulled me into his arms, which tamed the raging inferno within me so that it was almost bearable. "Baby girl, you're eighteen…"

I cut him off. "Am I getting my wolf?" I was both panicked and excited all at once. He smiled down at me, "Yes, I think so. It's okay, Kane will help alleviate the pain, I'll hold you as long as it takes."

"Your wolf can do that? Is it because you're an alpha?" I asked, but only moments later…

My wolf unfurled like a flash of light in my mind's eye. The air seemed to ripple and vibrate with its force, like the sound of a whip, snapping forward, connecting my wolf with his. A split-second burst of energy left a lingering echo, leaving everything around us feeling charged and electrified.

"Ezra, you found our mate." The magnificent creature said, bowing towards Bash's wolf, Kane, whom I could now see so vividly in my mind's eye. He was a mountainous beast, with a calico coloring of grays, whites, blacks, and browns. He was strong, yet beautiful as the moonlight, rained down on him, glinting off his fur.

His eyes were piercing, as he returned the bow to my wolf, **"Lana, at last we meet."** He spoke.

"Wha…what?" I asked as I tried to focus on the power and elegance of my wolf, "Lana?"

"Yes, Ezra. My name is Lana. The moon Goddess has paired us together, and I've been watching over you. I've wanted to meet you for a long time."

"Same," I said, tears now escaping my eyes.

CHAPTER TEN

THE GREENHOUSE.

--Bash's POV

I was stunned, at that moment. Kissing her was like nothing I could have ever imagined. It was explosive, like the igniting of a spark, setting off fireworks that danced in the night sky falling in waves around us, wrapping us in a blanket of love and ecstasy. A blanket, I was reluctant to crawl out from under.

I wondered what it would mean for us to just stay there. Our relationship up until now has been a rollercoaster. One minute, I was soaring high; the next, m m I was jolted sideways, my heart aching, and my mind disoriented. Everything about Ezra just drew me in. Every one of her quirks kept me on my toes, never knowing what was going to happen next. It was exhilarating but in the best possible way.

It took every ounce of strength I could muster, not to take her right there and then. To feel my teeth, sink into her flawless complexion, claiming her to be my Luna. But that wasn't a possibility, not now. I knew she needed time and space after what happened at the hospital. I could never forget the way she looked, as she tried desperately to get away from me.

Her words had sliced through my newfound joy in finding my mate, from the moments when relief washed over me, seeing that she was going to be okay, to the moment when I lost her all over again. *"I don't want you here."* I was trying to respect her wishes, to stay away from her.

That was until I saw her on Gabe's lap. I hate that guy. I hated him for touching her, in a way I longed to do. I hated him for the way she smiled at him. I hated him for putting his lips to her throat. The way he so arrogantly placed his hand on my mate's hip, claiming she was his. But she would never be his to claim.

I never could have predicted the events that would forever change my life. I can remember every moment leading up to the kiss. How sexy she looked sitting on my bike in front of me. Her bratty behavior as she pushed me to my breaking point. Every nervous thought, and eager yearning I felt when I saw her exposed skin, building up until I couldn't restrain myself any further.

I wanted to touch her, to feel her body against mine, to taste her lips. The pull was magnetic, drawing me closer to her until I became acutely aware that I no longer had control over Kane or my own body. My heart was beating so deeply in my chest, I could feel it in my throat, as Kane closed the distance between her lips and mine.

When our lips finally met, time froze, bowing to the glorious, fiery redhead in my arms. All I could feel was the softness and warmth of her lips. She was kissing me like she wanted me in the same way that I needed her, which excited my wolf further, Kane could already sense her wolf.

As our kiss deepened, it allowed her wolf to surface. A painful moment for young wolves, but our bond would help to lighten the burden. If anything, I could give her this, along with every part of my heart and soul. This was my mate, and nothing else mattered at that moment than the closeness of our bodies, as our souls mended together, forming an even stronger bond.

But her body was tired, and I needed to get her home, she needed to rest. It was time to pull off the covers.

"Babygirl, we need to go now," I said, still holding her in my arms, her legs were still wrapped around my waist, damn that felt so fucking good. I slid my hand under her ass and picked her up off the bike.

"Bash? Don't leave me, okay? I don't want you to leave."

"I'm not going anywhere, but you need to rest." I smiled at her words.

"You're always so bossy," she said with a big yawn.

"And you're a brat." I laughed.

"That's fair." She said returning my laugh.

As we walked through the crowd of people everybody was staring at us. This wasn't my first choice, but the only thing that mattered was what she needed, and right now that was sleep and lots of it. My dad had a suite here, so I went straight to the top floor. When I entered the room, I went straight to the king bed. I laid Ezra down, brushing her hair out of her still face.

"Do you think? I mean, I need these jeans off. They suck." She said shyly.

I took my shirt off, handing it to her. "You can sleep in this, and I'll have Kit bring you some clean clothes." She didn't take my shirt, she just sat there staring at my shirtless body. So, I moved closer to her, "Don't make me repeat myself, Ez."

"Yes, sir!" She said saluting me and then fell back down on the bed laughing.

I took my shirt and wrapped it around her hands in a quick movement, then pressed them down onto the bed above her head, pinning her body in place with mine, "You use it, or I will." I teased.

Her breath quickened, I watched her chest rising and falling, and I kissed down her neck and collarbone, before releasing her.

"Why'd you stop?" she suddenly asked, sitting up.

"Stop? I haven't even started, yet."

--Ezra's POV

I wanted him to touch me more, to kiss me more, but I was also so tired. And my head was beginning to hurt. No doubt, that was from the drinks I had earlier, and the intensity of getting my wolf. I picked up his shirt and went to the bathroom, I slipped off my very revealing outfit and slid into his still-warm shirt. I lifted the shirt to my nose. It smelled like him, and I found the scent intoxicating.

"Lana?" I asked my wolf.

"Hello Ezra," Lana's voice rang through my mind's eye, and it brought me some relief. I just wanted to make sure this was real and that you're here with me."

"Ezra, I won't be leaving you. Not now, not ever. I know you've felt alone for so long, but I have always been there. I know you have a lot of questions. I'll do my best to always answer them all for you. But for right now, we need our mate,"

I almost forgot about that declaration.

Bash was my mate.

"Okay," I said, exiting the bathroom. Bash was lying on the bed, and when I walked into the room, his eyes landed on me. I folded my hands together in front of me. I liked the way he looked at me, but it was something I still wasn't familiar with. "Does it look awful?"

"No. Babygirl, I like it better on you." He said, pulling the blankets down, allowing space for me to crawl into the bed with him. I crawled in, and he pulled me into his side. My head was lying on his exposed skin. There was hair across the top of his chest, and I couldn't help but rake my fingers through it. It didn't take long for me to fall asleep there in his arms. I don't think I had ever felt as safe as I did at that moment.

The morning came with a heavy ringing in my ears and an empty space beside me. I rubbed the sleep from my eyes and saw a piece of paper on the nightstand. I picked it up.

(Morning, Baby girl, I didn't want to wake you. Kit brought you some clothes, and they are waiting for you in the bathroom. There are two Tylenol on the stand; don't be stubborn; take them. Get showered and dressed then meet me on the roof.)

I set the note down, and picked up the Tylenol, swallowing them down with the glass of water also sitting there. I sat back down in the bed for a minute, "Lana?"

"Morning, Ezra."

"What do you think he's doing on the roof?"

"I don't know, but if you want to find out, you'd better get moving." She laughed.

I went to the bathroom, and sure enough, there was a stack of clothes folded on the bathroom sink. Next to it, there was a large supply of bathing products. I turned on the shower water and picked out the products I would need. I took off Bash's shirt, folded it, and placed it next to the other clothes.

The shower was warm as it ran down my body, and I could have stayed there in that steamy rain forever if I didn't have anywhere else to be.

I quickly cleaned up and got out. I picked up the clothes that Kit had brought for me. I slid on the jeans and looked at the shirt. It was one of my favorites, but instead, I picked up his shirt. I threw it back on and tucked it into the front of my jeans, before leaving the hotel room. Outside of the room, stood a burly-looking man. He smiled when he saw me, "You must be Ezra?"

"Yes, can I help you?"

"I'm, Dalton. I'm one of the Gamma for the Night Tree Pack. Alpha asked me to show you to the roof, whenever you woke up, if you're ready I can take you now," he was kind, but he looked annoyed that this was how his Alpha chose to utilize his position.

I nodded and he turned heading down the hallway. I followed him through a door at the end and up a flight of stairs. When he opened the door at the top, it revealed a large open space. The sun was beating down on the pavement, covering it with a bright sheen, the sudden brightness had my eyes squinting at first, but when they adjusted to the light, I saw that in the middle of the roof, there was a tall building made of glass. A greenhouse. I walked forward, and when I looked inside, I saw Bash.

Why does my heart always skip a beat when I see this guy? For real, this is a health hazard. He was standing in the middle of the greenhouse, wearing black jeans, a white V-neck T-shirt, and his signature black leather jacket.

In the middle of the greenhouse, sat a beautiful table with place settings for two. In the middle of the table sat a vase with a single rose in it. All around him, there were different plants and budding vines, bright colors, and amazing scents flooded my senses. I could feel my mouth gaping open at the wonder of it.

"Bash? What is this?" I asked moving closer to him.

"This? Just a perk of being an Alpha."

I knew he was the Alpha of the Night Tree Pack. But he had never actually said that before, and I was suddenly laughing at his words. It was easy to forget how important he truly was to our pack. When we were together, he wasn't my Alpha, he was just Bash. This slightly awkward and devilishly handsome guy. He was easily amused, and fun to be around. Caring at times, bossy at others, and always dependable.

"Are you laughing at me?" he chuckled.

"Well yeah, I mean. You? Alpha?" I said teasing him, I walked further into the greenhouse, touching and smelling the different variations of flowers and plants, committing the look and scents to memory. I had never seen anything so beautiful. Oakland had a lot of public parks, but they couldn't even begin to compare to this. Among the busy city streets and large buildings, it was hard to imagine feeling so grounded in nature.

"Do you like it?" he whispered into my ear, as he moved behind me, putting his hands around my waist. The moment his hands were on my body, I couldn't think of anything besides him and his body. Lana was whining now too; she wanted Kane as badly if not worse than I wanted Bash.

My body was trembling beneath his touch, but I managed to nod my head in response to his question.

"Use your words, Babygirl," he ordered, his voice deep and husky as he grabbed ahold of my hips, pressing them firmly back into him, and I could feel the hardness in his pants against my ass.

"It's beautiful Bash," I answered between breaths.

"Dalton, you can go, we'll be okay here," he said to the man still standing at the doorway of the greenhouse. Dalton nodded and moved out of the door and out of view. I looked at Bash, I had forgotten his Gamma was even there. But Bash, unbothered, undid the button on my jeans, moving one hand down to the wetness he had created while moving his other hand up to my neck, grasping it firmly, and I let him control my movements. A moan escaped me, which he leaned down and captured with his mouth.

This was what I needed. This was what my body had been craving since that first day when I met him. These thoughts had taken up residence in my mind since that first caress of his fingertips against my thigh on the bike. I had been denying myself because I didn't want to admit that I wanted him. But right now, I only had one thought. *I want more.*

He began rubbing his fingers in little circles, and it was a touch I had never experienced before. He kept going until my body began to shake and quiver under his touch, "Fuck, Bash!" I screamed as I reached my climax. My knees were weak, and I would have fallen if he didn't pick me up. He carried me over to the table, knocking everything to the ground as he sat me down on it. I was nervous as he knelt before me, pulling my jeans and panties down.

"Are you okay?" he asked, and I once again shook my head up and down. Nerves or not, I wanted him in a way that defied logic.

"Words, Babygirl." He said, looking up at me.

"Yes, I don't want you to stop."

"Good girl," he grinned as he pushed my thighs apart with his hands, then kissed down them until his tongue was gliding over my clit.

He let out a deep, throaty groan from between my legs, which only echoed my own desires. My eyes closed, and my hips ground against his face, in awe of the miracle he was performing with his tongue. Suddenly he stopped, sucking on my clit before breaking the suction, and it made me gasp. "Eyes on me, Ez." I looked down at him as he brought me to my climax a second time.

I was in complete ecstasy.

I was breathing heavily as he ran my panties back up over my legs. He helped me stand, as he pulled them up to my hip bones. Then he kissed me, before allowing me to lie against his chest.

"You're incredibly sensitive, Ez."

"Is that a bad thing?" I asked looking up at him.

"No, sweetheart, it's amazing, you're perfect.

CHAPTER ELEVEN

CUT ME, THAT'S NOTHING BUT A SCRATCH.

--Bash's POV

I barely slept last night. I watched as Ezra slept, peacefully draped over my chest. I wasn't sure how it happened, but she was finally mine. After six long months of emotional torment, I was finally holding her close. I had declared my true feelings for her, and even though her words were telling me she didn't feel the same, her actions spoke volumes. She had also been drinking though, and I wondered if when she woke up, once she realized what happened, if she would hate me for it. All that changed when I saw her walk into the greenhouse wearing my shirt. Seeing her refusing to relinquish it, made my wolf, Kane, hungry and possessive. The closer she got to me, the stronger that urge became. When I touched her, her arousal set off something primal within me.

Kissing her was fire, but tasting her as she reached her climax, the needy expression in her eyes as she looked at me, that was otherworldly. If I were any other wolf, and if she were any other girl, this would have been so much simpler. Most people find their mate, mark them, and that's, that. But Ezra wasn't just a girl, she saw the world in a unique way. She was careful and cautious, always hiding behind witty remarks and jokes. So much of her was still hidden away, and she wouldn't let me in. Whatever her life had been, it built up walls around her heart, and she wouldn't talk about it. Making loving her the hardest thing I've ever done.

I wasn't just any wolf either, I was the Alpha of Night Tree Pack, so marking her would make her our packs Luna, my Luna. She was barely eighteen, heavily guarded, and I knew I would have to wait to fully take her. Her face was still buried into my chest when she spoke, "Bash? What happens tomorrow?"

"What do you mean, Baby girl?" I asked, brushing her hair back out of her face, letting those baby blue eyes cut through me as she met my gaze.

"I mean, I'm your mate, but I'm not ready to be your Luna. What happens tomorrow when school starts, and everyone wants to know what this is? What are we going to tell them?"

"We can tell them, whatever you're ready to tell them, Ez." I knew I was ready; I would proudly claim this girl as mine if she'd let me, but something told me that wasn't going to be the case.

"Ez, you can talk to me, always," my voice was barely a whisper, "but I can't read your mind, and I can't help you, if you don't let me in."

She looked up at me, misty eyed, "I can't." she sobbed.

Once she started crying, she couldn't stop. I wrapped my arms tightly around her. I would hold her for as long as she would let me, and when she was ready to talk, I would listen.

"It doesn't matter what we do or don't tell people, does it Bash?" she finally said after her sobs had slowed down, "Everyone will talk, and they'll know."

"Yes, they'll talk. And they might even think they know, but none of that really matters Ezra, the only thing that matters now is us."

I was trying to listen to him, but I couldn't. My mind just kept telling me that I wasn't fit to be anyone's Luna. I could barely take care of myself, there was no way in hell, I could take care of our entire pack. I wanted to believe in his words. To believe in him. In us. That we were the only ones that mattered here, but it wasn't true.

"I never asked for this," I said, moving out of his arms. He was moving with me now; he knew I was planning to run. But he pulled me back in close to him, "I know, sweetheart, I know," he said as he bent down, placing his lips on mine. I loved the way he kissed me, but right now…I couldn't let myself think about that, right now, kissing him felt like a lie. The Moon Goddess had made a mistake, I wasn't meant to be his mate, or his Luna. I broke the kiss and put my arms up on his chest.

"Bash, I just, I need some time. Please."

"Of course, we have nothing but time here Ez. No one is pressuring you."

"Well, it doesn't feel like that." How could things go from amazing to terrifying in a matter of minutes?

"Just talk to me, Baby Girl, tell me what you're so afraid of, and we'll fix it together," his eyes were filled with sadness, and I couldn't bare to look at him any longer.

"I need to go. I'll call you later." I said moving out of his arms.

"I can take you home," he said, but I put my hand up to stop him, "No, I can get home on my own," I said.

"If you won't let me take you, then Dalton will drive you," he countered.

"No, Bash. I will take myself home, and you will send Dalton back to wherever he came from."

"Why must you always fight me?" he asked, his temper spiking. I didn't bother to answer him. I just kissed his cheek and then left. No words were going to fix this. Not right now.

I was walking for about five blocks when I realized there was a black car trailing me. It would park at the beginning of the block, and once I got to the next one, it would move forward and then park again. I wasn't sure who it was, but it was pissing me off.

I turned to the right, even though that wasn't the way to Kit's apartment. The building on the corner was large, with glass windows that scaled the height of the building. I leaned into it and waited for the car to turn the corner. When the car turned the corner, I took off running in the opposite direction. When I looked behind me, I saw the car doing a U-turn. Yup, this car was definitely following me.

As I ran, my adrenaline kicked in. It wasn't long before I heard Lana say, **"Shift, we can run faster that way."**

I didn't know how to shift. I had never done that; it hadn't even been a full day that I'd had my wolf, and the thought of shifting was one I hadn't had to deal with yet.

"I can't," I told her, as I turned to cut through an alleyway. I didn't make it a habit to run through alleys by myself, but as the saying goes, in desperate times, screw logic or whatever. Once I was safely in the Alleyway, I knelt behind a big dumpster, so that I couldn't be seen from the street. I was breathing fast and heavy. I wasn't paying attention. Lana growled, pulling my attention to the darkness behind me. There was a group of guys walking right toward me.

"What do we have here?" One guy asked.

"Seems like the Goddess gave us a gift, brothers," said another one. I stood back up and went to move around the dumpster when the third guy put his arm out in front of my chest, stopping my movement. I backed up against the wall again. *Well, this is bad.*

"Where do you think you're going, girly?" he asked.

"I don't want any trouble; I'm just trying to get home." My voice was strained, and I was already out of breath. There was no way in hell I was getting out of here.

"Well, you might not be looking for trouble, but you did find it," said guy one; he was laughing, and his cocky smile made my skin crawl. He was an older guy, and for some reason, his face looked familiar to me. The other two guys each grabbed ahold of my arms.

"Get off me," I shouted as I kicked one of them in the knee. He stumbled down grabbing it, but the other guy still had a firm hold on my arm. The first guy, the one with the cocky smile, pulled out a knife and held it up to my throat.

"Try anything like that again, and it'll be your last move," he whispered into my ear. He was trying to scare me, but in comparison to my own dad, this guy was nothing but a pup. I started laughing at the thought, and it pissed him off. He pressed the knife hard into my throat, "Shut up, you bitch."

I could feel the blade pushing through my skin and a warm liquid moving down my throat.

"Well, go on then," I said, provoking him further, "Cut me, that's nothing but a scratch."

It's not like I wanted him to do anything, but I heard worse threats in my life. I've suffered worse at the hands of my dad. So, fear of pain? That was something I no longer had.

"This bitch is nuts," said the guy holding onto my arm, "Let's just get out of here, I'm not tryin' to catch a charge today."

But the guy with the knife was staring at me, in a weird way. He removed the knife from my throat and then licked up the line of blood.

"You look sweet, and you taste sweet, but that mouth of yours is going to get you in trouble," he said, motioning for the other guy to let go of my arm. "Some guys might think you get off on the pain."

"Maybe," I said, then I pushed between the two guys and walked past them, "But I'm not interested in what you think."

"Hey, what's your name?" he asked.

"Yeah, you aren't getting my name, buddy." I didn't turn around. I kept walking until I was safely out of the Alley. As soon as I reached the street, that black car pulled up. It stopped, and the window rolled down.

"Miss Ezra, Bash is going to kill me if you don't get home safe, and since you seem to be good at finding trouble, can you please get in the car?"

"I should've known," I said, opening the door to the car and sliding into the back seat. I looked out the window and saw that older guy standing at the end of the Alley. He didn't take his eyes off me, as the car pulled away.

"We should swing by the hospital and get that looked at," Dalton said as he glanced up into the rearview mirror.

"I'm fine, Dalton. It's just a scratch," I answered, and he laughed, looking quite amused.

"What?"

"Well," Dalton chuckled, "I just didn't realize my future Luna was such a badass."

"I'm not." I corrected.

"Well, I'd say any girl who can get away from three thugs with only a scratch is pretty badass," he continued.

"I'm not arguing that point with you. I'm just not your future Luna, Dalton."

He pulled over the car then and turned to look at me. "Miss Ezra, it's not my place to say this, but sometimes those not looking to where the crown are the ones most qualified."

"I'm guessing that's a metaphor, right? Tell me there is no actual crown." I laughed.

"I'm sure we could probably make one," he joked as he threw the car back into drive.

"I'll pass," I said, rolling my eyes.

As we pulled up to Kit's house, he spoke again. "Miss Ezra, please think about what I said."

"Thank you for the ride, Dalton. And I will think about it, I promise." He nodded, and I got out, walking into Kit's.

When I got inside the house, Beth was sitting on the couch. She was giving me a death glare that I countered with a look of my own that said, "I'm not in the mood." She got up and stormed off to her bedroom. I didn't know what her problem was, but at this moment, it wasn't high on my list of priorities.

I went into Kit's room, and she was watching TV, she looked up at me and then sat up on the bed, giving me her best "Mom" impression.

"First off little lady, what happened to your neck? Second, that is not the shirt I brought you this morning. Third, what are you doing here? Aren't you supposed to be on a super romantic date with Bash?"

"First, it's nothing, just a scratch. Second, I know it's Bash's shirt. And third, I ran away." I sat down on her bed and kicked off my shoes.

"Ezzie? What's going on?" she asked genuinely concerned.

"I don't know, Kit. I like him."

She looked just as confused as I felt.

"Did something happen? How can liking him be a problem? You two are so cute together."

"Because, the Moon Goddess hates me, Kit. He's my mate," I said.

"Wait, back-up, rewind that shit, Ez. Did you get your wolf and not fucking tell me?"

I smiled at her, "Her name is Lana, and she's beautiful, her fur is red, and she's perfect. Except she's found her mate already, and it's Bash. It was weird. First, I was kissing him, and then…"

"Oh, my Goddess, he kissed you? And he's your mate? Damn, girl. This is big news; we need to celebrate!"

"No, Kit. He's, our Alpha."

"And?" she said, nudging me with her elbow.

"And I can't be his Luna. I'm not good enough."

"Of course you're good enough, Ezzie; you are the strongest person I know. And you're always taking care of everyone else, when are you going to do something for yourself?"

I grabbed her pillow. Holding it over my face, I screamed. I didn't know how to answer her question. Whatever she saw in me, it wasn't strength. Stubbornness. Maybe. But not strength. I was afraid of everything. I was weak. I didn't want to die, but I was also afraid to live. I simply existed in this life, and I hated myself for it.

CHAPTER TWELVE

"SLUT"

"Get your ass in the fucking car, Kit. We're going to be late," I yelled as she ran out of the house.

"We're fine, we have like…"

"Seven minutes, Kit. We have like seven minutes before we're late," I said, as I pushed the car door open for her to get in.

"Want me to drive?" she asked as she slid in.

"NO, I'd rather be alive when we get there." I laughed.

"I'm sorry, but this took some effort," she motioned to her outfit, which was great, I'll give it to her.

"Your outfit is amazing, Kit,"

"I know, right?" She said, tossing her hair behind her neck.

When we got to school, I had exactly two minutes to get to orientation, and I was thanking the Goddess that Kit's apartment was so close to campus. I was running so hard that when I finally reached the auditorium, I had little sweat beads gathering on my forehead. I think every person in the first-year class turned to look at me when I came running through the doors. I hurried and sat down in a chair near the back. Trying to fade in, people were already clicked up and they were whispering and quietly laughing with each other at my expense. It was awful. But that was just the beginning of this god-awful day.

After orientation, we got our class schedules. My first class was Art History with Professor Aryn. I was always good with numbers, so I decided to major in accounting, but I also enjoyed painting, so I chose creative electives. After that were Financial Accounting I with Professor Marcs, Principles of Macroeconomics with Professor Buell, and Calculus I with Professor Kizer.

I took my schedule and started making my way across campus to the Frick Fine Arts Building, for Art History. The whole walk there, different girls were giving me dirty looks, one girl even called me a slut as she walked past me. I didn't know what everyone's problem was. But it was pissing me off. I was excited when I finally saw a face I knew. Beth was in my art history class. When I went to say hi, she rolled her eyes at me and turned around. Something inside me snapped, I had had enough.

"What is your problem?" I asked, fuming.

"You are my problem," she said turning back towards me, "I was trying to be nice for Kit's sake, but you're not only a liar, you're also a fucking skank." Her eyes were glaring at me as she said it. Then another girl standing with her piped in, "She isn't even that pretty, I don't get it."

"Excuse me?" I asked, confused but also pissed off.

"You heard me," she said, throwing her hands onto her hips.

"Yeah, I heard the words, I'm just trying to make sense of them Beth."

"Everyone's talking about it, Ezra. What are you doing, trying to start a war? Gabe's pissed that Bash punched him out at his party, and all because you couldn't keep your legs closed."

Shit. I had been trying hard to forget about that party. I was so wrapped up in trying to figure out Bash, I never even thought about Gabe. Thankfully, I didn't have to respond to that, because Professor Aryn walked in, and ordered everyone to take a seat. That whole situation sucked, but just wait, it gets worse.

After class, I grabbed my stuff and left as quickly as I could, I instantly regretted saying anything to Beth. Because now I knew what all the whispers and pointing were about, and my roommate hated me because of it. Which meant this was going to be a long year. I was somewhere between punching a wall, and bawling my eyes out, when I entered Sennott Square, I turned the corner and ran straight into a hard body. Books went flying everywhere.

"Oh, my goddess, I am so sorry," I said as I crawled around trying to pick everything up.

"Ezra?"

I looked up, and of course, it was Gabe standing in front of me. He reached out a hand to help me stand up, I took it and handed him his books.

"Gabe, hey." I said awkwardly, "What are you doing here?"

"I have class, I was hoping to run into you, but it seems you beat me to it," he laughed.

"Yeah, again I am so sorry,"

"Don't be. It might be the best thing that's happened all day." He said, "Come on, I'll show you to class. Where are you heading?"

"Professor Marcs' class?"

"Sure, it's this way," he said.

"Oh, you don't have to walk me," I said, shooting him a friendly smile, which he returned.

"Well, you aren't getting rid of me that easily,"

"Oh no, I wasn't trying to…"

"Calm down, I was just joking with you, I want to walk you,"

"Thank you," I said, "So, business major?"

"Yeah, that's my dad's idea. He said it takes "good business sense" to run a pack. " He chuckled. Someday I'll have to run their hotel chain, too, so it was really the only choice."

"So, no future albums?"

"I love music. If it were up to me, I'd be studying music composition, but I guess there's this thing called "adulting" now? It's insane," his expression made me bust out laughing.

"Well, don't stop writing. Be adulty? Adulted? Adultish? Whatever, do that, but keep writing. Because, Gabe, your music is beautiful."

"If you're an English major, I'm going to lose it," he chuckled.

"Accounting, I like numbers," I said, shrugging.

"Well can I give you mine?" he asked.

"Give me what? Your number?"

"Yeah, or will your boyfriend punch me again?" he was laughing but his expression said so much more than his words did.

"Bash isn't my boyfriend." It wasn't a lie. Bash wasn't my boyfriend. I wasn't sure what Bash was other than my mate. We hadn't talked since I left the hotel, when I let him touch me in ways, that left my head spinning. I gave him my phone and he put his number in. When we got to Professor Marcs' class, a girl walked past us and gave me a dirty look. I rolled my eyes and took my phone back from Gabe.

"What was that?" he asked.

"We're fucking, and your posse isn't happy about it." I laughed.

"Oh shit, hope it was decent," he laughed.

"I wouldn't know," I laughed with him, then my cheeks instantly blushed. I was a virgin, but did he need to know that? No, so why did I just say that?

"Don't let them get to you, your smile is way too beautiful to be hidden away."

"Thanks, I should probably get in there," I said pointing to the classroom.

"Text me, so I can save your number, Ezra."

"Bye, Gabe."

"Later," he said before turning on his heels and strolling away. Even his walk was suave. I could see why all the girls liked him.

The rest of the day went by quickly, when I was able to go to the dining hall, I was happy to see Kit and Flynn sitting there. When Kit saw me, she waved me over.

"How's your first day going?" asked Flynn. She was always so nice; I don't think she had a mean or jealous bone in her body. I was happy that she didn't jump on Beth's hate-train.

"It's been, a day," I chuckled.

A girl at a table next to us "Coughed" the word "SLUT" towards me, and I sunk a little in my chair, but Kit was here, now. Which meant, this wasn't a shrug-it-off situation anymore.

She stood up pushing her chair backwards, "You have something you wanna say, bitch?"

The girl just rolled her eyes at Kit.

"Shut your fucking mouth, or I'll give you a reason to have your eyes roll." She said, before sitting back down at the table.

"Has that been going on all day, Ezzie?" she asked looking at me.

"It's okay, Kit."

"The fuck it is. I'll cut a bitch." She huffed. That made me feel better until Bash walked into the dining hall and v-lined straight toward us.

"Hi, Bash." Flynn greeted him.

"Hey, Flynn, right?" he asked making her smile.

"Yeah, you know who I am?" she asked.

"Of course I do, you're one of Ez's friends." He said now looking at me. It grew unbearably quiet until Kit grabbed her tray and stood up, "Well as fun as this is, I am going to go do something, somewhere else, that needs to be done," we all looked at her and then she added, "Come on Flynn, you can help." Flynn got the memo and followed Kit. It was far from subtle. But Bash sat down, glad to have me to himself.

"Can we talk?"

"Bash, I told you I need time."

"I know, but I miss you. I don't like being away from you like this."

"Well, I don't know what to tell you, Bash. Right now, I'm just really confused."

It was hard to look at him. He was so close, and I wanted him to touch me. My body was suddenly craving the feeling of his tongue against my clit. The way he gently massaged it, every sensation that it induced, and the way my heart sped up when he told me to look at him, *Fuck me*. I found that so sexy. It made me wonder what else he could do with his tongue, but those were selfish desires and thoughts. Ones I was trying hard to fight.

"You need to stop this, Ezra. He's our mate." Lana was now speaking to me; she'd been silent since I walked away from him. She and I were not agreeing on this, at all. She wanted Kane. Nothing else mattered to her. I wanted Bash, too. But there was so much more to it.

"I need to get to class, Bash. I'll call you later, okay," I said, grabbing my stuff and leaving before he could stop me.

"Turn around, go to our mate." Lana urged.

"I can't, Lana, okay?"

"He's hurting," she whined, clearly not happy about my decision.

All I could say, as I spared one glance over my shoulder was, "I know."

CHAPTER THIRTEEN

EZRA'S SONG

After classes, Kit and I went back to the apartment. We were sitting in the living room when Beth walked in. She threw her stuff down in the corner and went to the kitchen. Kit looked at me, confused. I didn't want Kit and Beth to be in a fight too, so I just shrugged my shoulders like I had no idea what was going on.

Kit got up and went to the kitchen to talk to Beth. And I switched on the TV. I was clicking through the stations. Nothing caught my interest until I clicked past the news channel, and I saw his face, again. It was the picture of the wanted man from before. Only, this time, I knew his face. It was the man from the alley.

I quickly grabbed my sneakers, put them on, and grabbed my phone. Then I returned to the Alley where I had last seen him, sneaking out before Kit could ask me where I was going. I'm sure this was the dumbest decision I had ever made, but I didn't want her to talk me out of it. When I got there, it was still daytime, but the Alley was dark. I was halfway down the alley when I heard a chuckle ahead of me.

I stopped walking. " Are you going to just stand there in the shadows?" I asked the chuckling man.

"Didn't expect you to come back here," he said, walking forward into the poorly lit Alley.

"I needed to talk to you."

"We have nothing to talk about, princess," he smiled, "But if you want to have some more fun…" he paused pulling out his knife and twirling it around his fingers, "I'd be happy to oblige."

"Princess?" I asked, stepping closer to him.

"Yeah, seems fitting,"

"I assure you; I'm no princess."

A sly grin spread across his face, "Should I just call you, playtime then?"

"My name is Ezra; you can call me that. And you? What's your name?"

He put his knife away and looked at me, "Junior, but I go by Juno."

"And why would you be a person of interest in a home burglary that never happened Juno?" I asked. He didn't answer, instead, he took off running. I darted after him, and I must have followed him for a mile or better before I lost him.

My lungs were burning as I bent over trying to catch my breath. Fuck, why didn't I take gym class more seriously? Still trying to catch my breath, I sat down on the curb and pulled out my phone. I typed Junior from Oakland, Pittsburgh into the search bar. Nothing, about this man showed up.

"Well, you aren't a cop," his voice startled me, and I jumped to my feet.

"Well, no shit?!"

"I had to be sure," he shrugged, "So who are you then?"

“I told you; my name is Ezra.”

“And what is it that you think you know?”

“I know you didn’t break into my house or nearly kill me.”

“No? But I did cut that pretty neck of yours, how can you be so sure?”

“Because my dad did!” I yelled my deepest, darkest secret at him. A total stranger, someone I knew nothing about. I immediately covered my mouth, shocked by my own words, which had just escaped them. What did I just do?

“Calm down, Princess. Let’s get some coffee.” He said, turning around and walking away. He didn’t seem to care if I followed him or not, and he didn’t even bother to look back in my direction.

Minutes had passed before I rushed to catch up to him. I kept asking him questions, but he stayed silent. I didn’t even know where we were going, but I wanted answers, and he had them. I followed him until, eventually, he went into an apartment building; it wasn’t a bad building or a bad neighborhood. It was close to the academy. It was small but nice.

When we got to apartment 6A, he put a key into the lock, and the door opened. He motioned for me to enter, and I did. He went to the kitchen and started a pot of coffee. Once it was brewed, he poured two cups and sat them down at the small table in the corner of the apartment without saying a word. Then he sat down at the table. I sat and took the other cup, staring at him.

“Now we can talk,” he said as he took a sip of his coffee.

"I don't understand," I finally said.

"Well, how would you when your father never told you," He kept looking at me in the same way he did in the Alley.

"Tell me what?" I was becoming more confused every minute I spent with this man, and I wanted answers. Not more puzzles.

When he spoke again, his tone was unmistakably sad. "My name is Juno Black, and I knew your mother. We were close once."

"You knew my mother?"

"Yes," he chuckled, "you know, you look like her. You have her hair, her blue eyes, and you even have her attitude. " He smiled as he talked about my likeness to my mother, and it made me feel more comfortable.

"So, you were friends? Do you know where she is now?"

He didn't answer my questions but instead asked one of his own: "What do you know about your mom?" He took another sip of his coffee, waiting patiently for me to answer. It felt like there was something I was missing, but I told him the truth.

"I remember how happy she always pretended to be. I remember her always protecting me from my dad, and I know that for whatever reason when she left, she didn't take me with her; she abandoned me," I answered.

"Your mother didn't abandon you, Ezra. She loved you with every fiber of her being." He sounded so sure, but I didn't believe him. If she loved me, she wouldn't have left without me. I must have done something to make her leave me with that monster of a man I called Dad. I hated myself for being so unworthy of my mother's love. But I hated her more. I hated her, and I loved her, and I missed her.

"She left me," I said, as tears were forming at the edges of my eyes. I wiped them away as he leaned forward.

"She loved you." He said with finality.

"Then why did she leave me there?" I shouted at him.

His expression had changed. He wasn't that cocky guy I had met in the Alley, and he wasn't the silent man I had followed here, his expression now made him feel familiar. This was the first time I had ever talked about my mom. The first time I admitted out loud, what my dad had done to me. All to someone I didn't even know.

"Your mother didn't leave you, Ezra."

"SHE DID!" I yelled again, "She fucking left me, and it was it is. I don't care, tell me about why my dad wants your head."

"I'm trying to, but you aren't listening," he said standing up from the table and walking to the apartment door, "Maybe you should go."

I stood up, kicked the chair back behind me, and moved towards him. "No! I need to know, and I'm not leaving until I get the answers I came for!"

He put his hand to my throat, pushing me back into the wall. A gasp escaped me, and then he looked me in the eyes and said, "We're done, now go."

He swung the door open, releasing me from his grip. I just stood there staring at him. "Go," he said again. His tone now, made me fearful. So, I slowly walked past him and out of the door, just in time to hear it slam shut behind me.

As I walked home, I thought about everything that had happened. **Junior Black.** That name sounded familiar to me. I couldn't remember why, and I was thinking so hard that my head hurt. *Ding* I reached down and pulled out my phone.

(Where are you?)

I shook my head, I didn't know what Bash wanted, and I didn't care. *Ding*

(Ezra, tell me where you are)

Goddess, how could you both want someone and want them to leave you alone? That was Bash for me, though. I loved being with him, but I hated his persistence, sometimes.

(Bash, I'm fine. I'm heading home now.)

(Where are you?)

(Why do you want to know? I'm allowed to leave my house, Bash. I don't owe you or anyone else an explanation)

(I know. But I came over to check on you, and Kit said you just left.)

(What part of time and space don't you seem to understand?)

(I just care, Ez.)

(Well STOP. I don't want you to.)

I wasn't sure if I truly meant that, but I knew right now he was pissing me off. *Ding* I wanted to scream. If I heard one more…

Ding

FUUUUUUUCK, for heaven's sake.

I looked at my phone, but it wasn't Bash. I opened the messages.

(Ezra's Song.

"In the depths of the morning, as the sun begins to rise, I think of you, Dear Ezra, and those bright blue eyes. You will never walk alone, for I will guide your stride, you and me together, side by side."

"I want to dance with you, in the silver glow of the moon, as the world fades away, in a dream come true. You are mine, sweet love; together, we'll soar high, but only with me will you touch the endless sky. In this journey of love, with every step we trace, know it's you, Dear Ezra, who belongs in my embrace."

Know that it's you, dear Ezra, who makes my heart race.)

(I'll never stop writing for you. -Gabe)

As I read through the messages, I realized I was in awe of Gabe. He wrote me a song and it melted away all the rage I was currently feeling for my mate. It filled my heart, instead, with a calmness I didn't feel with Bash. But it was the second message that made my heart beam.

CHAPTER FOURTEEN

THREE RULES.

--Bash's POV

I was going crazy. I couldn't think. I couldn't sleep. I didn't want to be with her, I needed to.

"Maybe you need to just trust her and give her some time," Zayne said, and it infuriated me. This wasn't about trust. She gave me a small taste of her, and I was in withdrawal. I had wanted her for so long, to have her dangled in front of me, baiting me and my wolf.

"She's mine, Zayne," I growled through clenched teeth.

"Is this girl really worth all this suffering?" Zayne asked. He's been my best friend since we were kids, but the more he spoke, the more vividly I imagined his last breath.

"Don't test me," I gnarled—the rage building within.

"Look, don't bite my head off. I'm just saying, look at you. You need to get control of yourself. She's doing more harm than good here. I want my friend back." His eyes were pleading, and they spoke volumes. I managed to pull my wolf back, which was on the brink of taking complete control.

"I'm sorry, Zayne. You might be right." I said, patting the back of his shoulder.

"Bro, there's a boat party down on the river. Let's go tonight. You need to get out of this apartment. And I need to get drunk."

"Yeah, fine," I said as I went to the bathroom. A cool shower would help temper Kane. He was pushing me to go to Ezra, but I've learned that was a bad idea. A drink or two might also help to calm Kane.

When we got to the River, I realized this was not a boat party. It was a yacht party. My yacht. *For fucks sake,* "Zayne? I'm throwing this party?" I looked at him, annoyed.

"Fuck yeah, you are. Which means you can't just leave, Buddy." He was laughing as he wrapped his arm around my shoulders and pulled me down the dock.

The party was raging, bottles were popping, and I was trying my best to stay in Alpha mode. I went down to the back deck and saw Beth; she was sitting with a group of girls, laughing and drinking and being, well, Beth. I knew her well; she was the closest thing I had to a relationship before I met Ezra. I scanned the group of girls but didn't see Ezra among them. Still, I figured I should say hi.

"Hey," I said as I approached, "Everyone, having a good time?"

"Alpha!" they all said in unison. Which was as impressive as it was cringy.

"Hey Beth," I said as I ran my finger under her chin, causing a rosy blush to appear on her cheeks.

"It's been a while, Bash. You've been so busy with your new little she-wolf, that I was feeling neglected." Beth was Zayne's little sister. Their dad was the previous Beta before I took over as Alpha, and Zayne took over as Beta. She was a spoiled little princess. But she had a nice body, and she never said no. I had made use of her to satisfy my needs last year. It wasn't like we dated. She would come over at night, but I never let her stay. I knew she would never be my Luna, and I didn't want her to get the wrong idea.

She wrapped her arms around my neck and moved her body in a swaying motion. I grabbed her arms firmly and removed them. This pissed her off, "I wanna dance!" she whined.

"I just came to say hi, Beth." She grabbed my hand and tried to pull me away from the group of girls. It was funny. She thought she had some control over me. But she didn't. The only girl who could bend me at their will was Ezra. *It will always be Ezra.*

"Can we please just talk?" she pleaded. I grabbed a glass of champagne from the waiter who was walking past and threw it back.

"Five minutes, Beth."

"You never used to have that issue," she laughed. She was drunk and getting on my last nerve.

"You're talking to your Alpha," I reminded her as I followed her to the far end of the deck. I leaned back into the railing and then gave her my attention.

"Five minutes, Beth. Use it wisely," I told her.

"Why do you hate me?" she asked, looking up at me.

"Beth, I don't hate you. I just don't want to date you." I corrected her.

"That bitch doesn't even want you!" she yelled, drawing everyone's attention to us. My patience was already wearing thin when Zayne approached us. Out of respect, I told him in a hushed voice that he should take Beth to lie down because it was clear she had drunk too much.

"Come on, Beth. Let's go inside," he told her as he took her arm.

"No! Five minutes, Bash," she said, fighting against her brother's grip.

"Beth, if you can't watch your tongue, things will end very badly for you," I said firmly.

"Bash!" Zayne cut in, "Come on, it's Beth," he was not happy about my threat to his sister.

"Get her inside, Zayne," I ordered him.

"Beth, let's go," he said, ushering her off the main deck and inside.

"Everything is good here," I told everyone, "Come on, is this a party or what?! Let's have some fun!"

We were passing under the Fort Pitt Bridge—the same bridge where Ezra had thrown my secret over the edge on my twenty-first birthday. I felt so close to her that day, but the distance between us now hurt even deeper as I remembered her red curls bouncing around as she twisted the pretend lock on her beautiful lips. I grabbed a bottle of whiskey and chugged.

"You aren't going to the Yacht party?" Beth asked Kit.

"I have a lot of homework." She said, shrugging her shoulders, "Maybe Ezra will go with you." She answered by pretending to gag herself with her finger. That about summed up our relationship anymore.

"I have other plans tonight," I spoke. Ignoring Beth completely.

"You aren't going to Bash's party?" she asked, suddenly interested in what I had to say.

"No, Beth, I've told you before. We are just friends. Which means I can do things, like not go to his stupid parties." I was surprised when I heard about it. Part of me was happy that it seemed like he was moving on from me and living his life. The other part of me was upset that he could move past us so easily. I had no right to feel that way because I was the one pulling away. Not him. But it didn't stop it from hurting.

"So, what are you doing tonight?" Beth asked.

"Why do you care?"

"I don't," she said turning around to leave.

Once she had left, I looked at Kit. She just put her hands up, "Leave me out of it. I'm Switzerland." She laughed. Which made me laugh, too.

"Love you, Kit. I'll see you later," I kissed her forehead and when I turned, she smacked my ass. "Love you too, girl. Make bad decisions!!! And have FUN!"

When I pulled up to the aquarium. There were no cars anywhere. But Gabe was standing out front, dressed in a designer two-piece suit that was tailored to his build, and a green button-up that matched his eyes. His belt pulled the look together. He was holding a single rose. When I got to him, he held out the rose for me to take.

"Thank you," I said taking the rose and smelling it, "It's beautiful."

"Are you ready?" he asked. I looked around at the empty parking spaces again.

"Um, I don't know how to tell you this Gabe, but I'm pretty sure it's closed," I laughed.

"Not for us," he said pushing the door open.

"Are we breaking and entering?" I asked half-joking.

Arching his brow at me, he asked, "Why, does that excite you?"

"Oh yeah, I'm a total badass," I said as I entered, the aquarium.

"I bought it for the day, Ezra. We get the whole place to ourselves."

"You did what? Are you kidding me?" I was slowly walking through, looking at all the various kinds of aquatic animals. It was surreal. As we moved through the different exhibits, the vibrant colors and graceful movements of the different fish and sea creatures had me mesmerized. Gabe stayed at my pace, allowing me to take in every new wonder, without any complaints. When we got to the jellyfish exhibit, the light seemed to reflect off their bodies. I watched them drift and pulse through the water and it was magical.

Once we made it to the middle of the aquarium, it got even better. There was a picnic set up in front of the most enormous tank I had ever seen, he had put so much thought into this day, and it was perfect. We sat, talked, and flirted with each other as the fish swam around us. After we ate, we continued walking through the aquarium. There was a tunnel through one of the tanks. As we moved through it, it felt like we were stepping into an underwater dream, but I wasn't looking at the fish; I was looking at Gabe.

He looked so good, and I couldn't stop admiring him. We stood there in our secluded sea for a moment, and a warmth rose in my cheeks when he caught me looking at him. Unspoken words lingered in the air between us, and I bit my bottom lip, unsure of what to say.

Suddenly, Gabe grabbed my hands and interlocked his fingers with mine. He lifted them above my head, securing both hands against the glass. He held both my wrists in one hand while he used his other hand to trace lightly down my arm and side before lifting the bottom of my blouse. My breath hitched as he ran his hand up under my shirt. His soft touches on my stomach were exhilarating. My heart was racing as he whispered in my ear, "I want you."

I shook my head, giving him silent permission to do whatever he wanted. He released my hands, his hand wrapping firmly around my throat, turning my head with his thumb, so he could kiss down my jawline. "Rule #1. Use your words, Kitten. That's especially important do you understand?" I went to shake my head, and he stopped kissing me. "Rule #2. Three strikes and that ass is mine. That's strike one, Kitten. Words."

"Yes," I said quickly, the raspiness in his voice was turning me on, as much as his grip around my throat, which had my pussy pulsating, begging for his touch.

"Rule #3. We go at your pace, if you aren't comfortable, or you're hurting, you need to tell me."

"Gabe?"

"Yes, Kitten?"

"You're…my, my first."

A low growl escaped him, and he licked his lips like I was the tastiest snack he'd ever seen.

"Do you want this, Kitten?" I could feel the girthy length of his cock, as his body pressed against mine. The tension built up between us as I dissected his words. My breathing was uneven, and it was hard to concentrate on anything other than giving in to his wants and desires.

"I want you," I assured him.

He stepped back as a sexy grin spread across his face. He took off his suit jacket, setting it to the side. Even the way he took off his jacket was sexy. He slipped his belt off, untucking his shirt. "Do you trust me?" he asked, and I was growing impatient—so many questions, when all I wanted was more touches. I shook my head again, forgetting the first rule. He arched his brow at me again. "Strike two, Kitten."

"Yes, I trust you," I corrected myself.

"Good girl, now turn around." I did as I was told, he slid the belt around my wrists, tightening it around them. He slid my panties off, but then he froze. "Ezra? What is this?" I was so aroused that I completely forgot about my scars.

"It. It's nothing," I said, suddenly feeling ashamed and embarrassed. I spun around so that my naked ass was now pressed against the glass, shielding it from his view.

"Who did that to you? Tell me. Now." He ordered. The sexy raspiness in his voice had disappeared, replaced with confusion and agony, "Was it Bash? I'll fucking kill him." He breathed.

"No!" I quickly cut him off, "It wasn't Bash; I've never…he doesn't know," I was crying now; my hands were still secured behind me, and I couldn't wipe away the tears. Gabe reached up, wiping them from my cheeks. The look in his eyes was pained as he pulled me into him and kissed me. Deeply, passionately, possessively. He drowned my sorrows with his tongue as he sucked in my bottom lip. When he pulled away, his hands were on either side of my face. He stroked my cheeks with his thumbs as he leaned his forehead into mine.

"I'm so sorry, I crossed a line, I wasn't thinking," he said.

"Gabe?"

"If I pushed you too much, Ezra…I didn't know."

"I'm okay, Gabe; I want this; I want you to do this. Please...Unless you don't want me anymore. I get it."

"I want you, but I can't. This changes everything. The way I fuck, it's rough."

"I know. I also know you won't hurt me. I trust you. Now, trust me."

I wasn't sure what he was thinking, and I hated it. The silence between us made me nervous, and I bit my lip. He smacked my cheek lightly. "Those are mine," he said, and relief washed over me. Do that again, and I won't be able to resist."

Challenge accepted. I thought as I asked, "What? This?" and then I bit my lip again.

He tangled his fingers in my hair, pulling my head back, and a needy moan escaped my lips. "you're playing a dangerous game, Kitten," he warned, "Are you going to behave for Daddy?"

"Maybe, maybe not?" I wanted to see how far I could push him; he was steeping with desire as he forced me to kneel before him.

He undid his pants and freed his large erection. I was suddenly incredibly nervous. He was huge.

"Eyes on me, Kitten." I turned my head up to look at him and was met with his deep, possessive tone, "Good girl," he said as he guided my head forward. I liked the satisfied sounds he made when I wrapped my mouth around his cock. He guided me on and off slowly. He wasn't going deep, but I could feel him hit the back of my throat. He increased the speed and then pushed in farther, gagging me, "Fuck," he said as he pulled me off him, studying my face as I looked up at him, tears forming in the corners of my eyes from being gagged. But I liked it, and I hoped he could tell.

"Are we going to behave?" he asked again.

"Yes."

"Yes, who?"

"Yes, Daddy," I said.

He lifted me easily into a standing position and turned me around, gripping my throat as he began rubbing my clit lightly, "Fuck, Kitten. You're so wet." He said as he slid his fingers down between my lips. He brought his fingers up to his mouth, sucking my cum from them. Then he turned my face, kissing me so I could taste it too.

"Do you want Daddy's cock?" he asked, and I shook my head yes, knowing damn well I was breaking the rules. The deep growl that escaped him as he said, "Strike three," was all I needed to know. He pulled down on the belt. My back arched up, and he pushed me forward so that I was bent over as he smacked my ass.

"Bad girls, get spankings," he said as he smacked my ass again, "Is this what you want?"

"No, I want to feel you," I said as my pussy tightened, and my body began quivering; I needed him; I needed him like a wolf needs a moon and like a world needs a sun. Like the night needs the stars. I needed him so bad I was in tears, "Please, Daddy, please, I need you!" I begged.

"That's my good girl," he said as he finally thrust in me, "Fuck, Kitten. You're so tight," he hummed, then he smacked my ass again.

"This is my ass, you understand?" he asked.

"Yes, Daddy," I barely got the words out before he thrust again.

It hurt, but I didn't want him to stop.

He thrust again as he grabbed ahold of my hips, slamming his cock so far into me I might have been seeing stars, and then his pace increased, hard and deep.

I was screaming out as a mix of pleasure and pain enveloped me. He didn't stop until I reached my climax, my body quivering, and then he pulled out finishing in his jacket.

He released my wrists from the belt, and sat down, pulling me into his arms. There was blood all over his cock, and a trail of it rolling down between my thighs.

"Fuck, Ezra. Are you okay?" he asked as I cuddled into him.

"I've never felt better," I laughed, and a smile crept onto his face.

CHAPTER FIFTEEN

SAY THE WORDS, KITTEN.

I woke up the following day in a bed I didn't recognize. But the sheets were silky against my skin. Lying next to me was Gabe. I tried to sit up, but everything hurt. So, I decided against it, I snuggled into his side, and he wrapped his arm around me bending down to kiss my forehead, without even opening his eyes.

"Morning, Kitten," he said. Before letting his head fall back down on the pillow. This was not like my night with Bash, when I woke up all alone in bed, and I was so happy he was still there.

"Where are we?" I asked, "I don't remember…"

He chuckled, "You fell asleep on me at the aquarium. I brought you back to my place."

"I…Oh, my Goddess, I'm so sorry," I began but he shushed me.

"No more apologies, Ezra," he said as he tangled his hand in my hair, pulling me into a kiss. This was the second time he shut down my self-doubt with a kiss, and I wasn't hating it. When the kiss broke, I was breathless again. And I wanted more, I ran my hand down his abs towards his cock, but he grabbed my wrist. "No, Kitten," he said as he brought my hand to his lips, gently kissing my fingers.

"But…"

"I said no. Are you disobeying me?" His brow rose as he looked at me.

"No. I just don't understand," I said as I sat up, but the pain hit me hard.

"You need rest, and you need to heal. I hurt you, Ezra." His voice broke as he said that last part, and I could tell he was upset. "You broke rule #3," his eyes were darker as he looked down at me. Wait. Was he upset with me?

"I didn't know," I said, looking up at him, "I mean, it hurt. But it also felt so good, and I didn't want you to stop."

"It was your first time, and I should've been gentler. In the future, I need you to tell me, is that understood, Kitten?"

"Yes."

"Yes…What?" he asked, his head cocking to the side.

"Yes, I understand." I corrected.

"Will you stay here with me?"

"Here? Like at your house?" I wasn't sure if he could hear the worry or the panic in my tone.

"Yes, Kitten. I'd like to be able to take care of you," he said as he ran his fingers around my belly button, something he's done a lot, and it was beginning to bring me comfort.

"Yes, I will stay with you."

"Good, girl. Now, try to rest. I'll get some of your things."

"Can you go later? I just want you here with me, while I fall asleep."

"Sure, I can go later," he pulled me back into him and ran his fingers through my hair until I fell back asleep.

I stayed with Gabe for the rest of the weekend. I loved being there with him, he gave me his undivided attention. It was like a dream come true. But I had school tomorrow, so I needed to go back to reality. I was going to miss him and the "us" that blossomed here. The way it felt to be cuddled up in his arms as we watched movies and the "accidental" popcorn fight that had taken place during them. The way we laughed and the way he smacked my ass as I danced in the kitchen, making him breakfast. All of it. Every single moment.

"You don't have to go, Kitten. You could stay," he said as I began packing my things into my suitcase.

"I'd love to just live in this moment with you, Gabe. But we have school, and I have work, so I should go…" He picked me up, causing me to scream playfully as he laid me down on the bed, pressing his half-naked body against me. "I wish I could just tie you up and keep you here all to myself."

"I like the sounds of that," I teased. He hasn't touched me since our date. He said I needed to heal, but that didn't stop him from driving me crazy.

"I'm serious, Ez. What if you just moved in?"

"Gabe, I can't, I'm renting a room with Kit and the girls, and it wouldn't be fair for them," I said reaching up to touch the side of his face. He turned his head to kiss my palm. He was always so affectionate, and I was going to miss that.

"I'll pay your rent, Ez. It won't affect them at all."

"I can't ask you to do that." I laughed.

"You didn't ask, but I'd do anything if it meant you would stay," he started kissing down my neck, and I moaned as they trailed down towards my breasts. My body moved instinctively beneath him, my legs wrapping around his waist. His kisses stopped, his lips were just far enough from my body that I could feel his warm breaths against my skin, and my back arched, trying to get closer to him. "Just think of all the fun we could have if you were here, Kitten." He spoke while he pulled my tank top down, exposing my breast. Sucking my nipple into his mouth and releasing the suction as he pulled his mouth away. My heart was racing. I've wanted this all weekend.

He spoke again, his voice low and raspy, "in the morning," now his hands were exploring my body, "after school," he bit my nipple, and I gasped, "Anytime, all you would have to do is ask, Kitten."

"Fuck, Daddy, please…"

"Please what, Kitten?"

"Please don't stop, I need you," a cocky smile spread across his face as he stood up, pulling his boxers down to reveal what I was longing for, "Stay with me, Kitten. And Daddy will take care of you."

"Okay," I said as I sat up, reaching towards his cock, he smacked my hand away, "Say the words, Kitten."

I sat back down on the bed, "I'll stay with you, Daddy."

Then he grabbed my legs and pulled me to the edge of the bed, giving me what I so desperately wanted, again.

A few hours later, I went back to the apartment and began packing my things. I didn't have many things, so it wasn't going to take me long. As I finished up, I left a note on Kit's bed.

(Don't be mad, but Gabe asked me to move in with him, and I said yes. I'll still pay for my part of the rent, so you won't have to worry about that. I love you. -Ezra)

Gabe and I were in the middle of eating dinner when my phone buzzed. I picked it up and it was a message from Kit.

(Girl, are you insane? You can't just move in with a man you just started seeing!)

"Kitten?" Gabe was looking at the phone in my hand, "Everything okay?"

"Yeah, it's just Kit," I said, turning the screen off and setting it down on the table. But it buzzed again. When I went to pick up my phone, Gabe grabbed it. "Let's eat Kitten, you can message your friend later."

"She's worried about me," I said, "I just want to let her know I'm okay."

He slammed his fist into the table. Which made me jump. I didn't understand why he was mad. Noticing the way I jumped, his face softened. "I just want to enjoy this meal with you, Kitten. Without interruptions. You can call her, after, Okay?"

"Okay, you're right. I should have turned my phone off, I'm sorry." I answered.

He got up and silently walked around the table, picked me up, and carried me to the bedroom. "Gabe? What are you doing? What about dinner?" I asked as he sat me down on the bed.

"Kitten, I told you no more apologies," he said as he opened the closet. Revealing a huge walk-in, that held an organized assortment of toys and restraints. I got off the bed and walked over to the closet, taking it all in. "What is all this?" I asked looking up at him.

"Most are meant, to please you Kitten, but some of them…are meant for disciplining."

"You want to discipline me? For texting my friend at dinner?"

"No, Kitten. I want you to be a good girl and listen,"

I walked into the closet and began looking at and touching everything in there. I wasn't sure how I felt about this. I was a little scared, I think. But at the same time, I wanted to know what he was capable of. Somehow, he had taken the violence I once feared and turned it into a pleasurable experience. With him, I didn't want to be in control. I didn't want to fight with him. I wanted him to do whatever he wanted because it felt so good when he did.

"Daddy?" I asked looking up at him, "I'm a little scared."

"Come here, Kitten," he said holding out his arms to me, and I melted into his embrace. "You're such a good girl, thank you for telling me."

"Can you show me?" I asked looking up at him. He picked me up and threw me over his shoulder, then smacked my ass, before grabbing something off the wall and walking back to the bed.

"Are those chains?" I asked. As he flipped me down on the bed.

"Pick a safe word, Kitten. If it gets to be too much, you say that word, and I'll stop," he removed my clothes and began fastening the chains around my arms and ankles, one at a time. Stopping after each one to ask if they were too tight. When I shook my head no, he growled, and I corrected myself by saying, "No."

He was so caring in every action; I couldn't imagine how he could punish me. He attached my hands to anchors that I hadn't noticed were installed in the bed frame.

"What is your safe word, Kitten?" he asked as he firmly pressed my legs apart, exposing my pussy to him, and attached the chains around my ankles to the bottom of the frame.

"Nemo," I said smiling. Since I lost my virginity to him, in an aquarium, I thought it was fitting.

He chuckled, "Okay, Nemo it is."

He slowly unbuttoned his shirt, tossing it to the side. When he left his pants on, I began to pout. He walked around the side of the bed, gripping my face as he leaned down, kissing me before releasing my face.

"I'll give you a reason to pout," he said as he blindfolded me.

Nothing happened for a while, and I was getting antsy. I began moving my body, trying to somehow feel him, but there was nothing until something cold began gliding down between my breasts. I shivered, the hairs standing up on my arms, as it trailed down, circling my belly button before resting on top of it. He picked it up with his mouth, I could feel his lips against my skin, and I moaned. "Daddy?"

"Do you like that, Kitten?" he asked.

"Yes, Daddy," Then it was gliding against my nipples, making them harden as the cool liquid melted, running down around them. He licked it up with his mouth. Suckling on my nipples, as a warm wetness began dripping out of my pussy.

"Are you Daddy's good girl?" he asked, as he pinched and pulled on my hard nipples. I didn't say anything but instead bit my lip. His hand was around my throat, "Strike one, Kitten. I told you; those are mine," his voice was growing deeper, more intense. I was pushing him. And enjoying every second of it.

After minutes of heavy breathing and exhales, his hand was on my thigh, tracing gently up toward the budding flower between my legs. But his touch was gone before he got there. Causing me to twist and moan in agony.

"You're not daddy's good girl, is that it? You want Daddy's cock, don't you? You dirty little slut."

"Yes, Daddy," I said, my body was craving what only he could give me. And then his fingers were gliding in me, pounding my pussy hard until a warm liquid gushed out, soaking my inner thighs and ass. "What a mess you made, Kitten." As I heard him licking his fingers.

"Please Daddy, I want to touch you…" I said as I pulled against the restraints.

"No touching, that's reserved for my good girl, but you're a dirty slut. You'll take what I give you, understand?"

"Ugh, Daddy!" I screamed.

"Do you remember your safe word?" he asked.

I shook my head yes. "Strike two Kitten."

He smacked my pussy then, and it shocked my body. "What do you want?"

"I want you!" I shouted.

"And whose pussy is this?" he asked, and I could hear him unbuckling his belt.

"It's yours, Daddy. It's your pussy, now please! I need you. Please, I'm begging you!" I was nearly crying now. My pussy was throbbing so badly, so needy for him, it hurt.

When I felt the tip of his cock, rubbing against my clit, I cried out again, he moved his hands under my ass, lifting my hips, and then he gave me my release.

When he was done, I started crying. It felt so good, and I loved every second of it, but needing him that badly hurt in a way I had never experienced. He quickly released the chains on my legs and then pulled the blindfold down as he released my hands. Then he pulled me into his chest before picking me up and carrying me to the shower. He started the water and kissed my forehead. "Are you okay?"

"I think I'm in love with you," I blurted out, which made him happy. He looked at me with gentle eyes. "You're mine, " he said, and I kissed him.

CHAPTER SIXTEEN

THE ONE TRUE, ALPHA

--Bash's POV

"KIT!" I yelled, running to catch up with her. She stopped and turned around.

"Oh, hey, Bash," she said as I reached her.

"How is she?" I asked, which didn't seem to surprise her at all. It's been weeks now, and Ezra still hasn't talked to me. She had moved in with Gabe, practically disappearing in the process. I couldn't speak to her because he was with her every time I saw her. Everything in the universe was screaming that she was done with me. I wanted to see her. I wanted to talk to her, but I was scared it would confirm my biggest fears. So, instead I watched her from afar.

"I don't know, Bash, I told you. She barely even responds to my messages anymore."

I wasn't the only one hurting; Kit was hurting, too. Her face was a canvas of emotional pain. Painted there for everyone to see. Her eyes were red and swollen as if she'd done nothing but cry since Ezra had left. Tears still brimming the edges. Her lips trembled as she tried to hold back the sobs that threatened to break loose. Deep furrows marked her brow, each line telling stories of anguish.

"I'm sorry, Kit," I said as we continued walking to class.

"You know what sucks the most?"

"Loving someone who doesn't love you back?" I answered, although I was sure that it was a rhetorical question.

"No." she said, stopping and turning to me, "and for what it's worth, I think she does love you, Bash. I just don't think she knows how to deal with it."

"I miss her," I said, and she agreed, "I miss her too, and that's what sucks. I feel like I lost my best friend. We've never been apart this long before."

I wrapped my arms around her, feeling the need for comfort just as much as she did. Having Ezra and losing her was a pain only Kit understood.

"I'll talk to you later, Bash." She said, breaking the hug and giving me a half-smile before walking off.

"Bro, who the fuck is that?" Zayne asked, running up to me from behind.

"Kit."

"That's Ezra's friend? Dude, she was in tears. What did you do to her?"

"It wasn't me Zayne, it's Gabe. He took her away from everyone, not just me." I was annoyed. I was pissed. I was…ready to start a war.

Enough was enough. And I was done standing idly by. It was time to take back what was mine.

"This is going to end now. I am going to get her back, Zayne. Even if it threatens the very existence we live in."

After classes, I would call a meeting in the Pack House, summoning all the Elders. It's been hundreds of years since there has been a war among our packs. The peace treaty established between my great, great grandfather and the werewolf counsel bound our three clans.

There were…Politics now. Still, taking another Alpha's mate, regardless of whether that bond had been fully established. It was a line that Gabe dared to cross, and now he would pay the price for crossing me. I wanted to tear him limb from limb. But retaliation from the Silver Pack for the murder of their Alpha could put my pack members' lives in danger. It would put Ezra's life in danger. So, I would play by the rules. For now.

Of course, that was only if I got caught.

No. No. As much as I wanted to rid the world of that filth. There had to be another way.

Zayne and I went straight to the packhouse after our final class, which just happened to be Combat and Shifting. This used to be my favorite class. I was easily one of the strongest wolves in class. All Alpha and Beta students took this class. Along with all Gamma or warrior wolves.

When I walked in, my eyes found Gabe and narrowed in on him. He wore a cocky grin on his face, and I had to swallow hard to keep Kane from killing him there and then.

"Bash, hey. Thomas and I were just talking. Maybe you can clear this up for us. I heard your pack is planning on replacing you. Any truth to that?"

"You and I both know damn well; I'm not replaceable."

"I don't know. I think your little mate might disagree with you." He laughed.

"Not here. Not now, Bash. Settle it on the mat." Zayne was speaking well, words that, at this point, meant nothing. I couldn't take my eyes off Gabe.

"Leave her out of this," I growled.

"I'd love to, but feel free to correct me if I'm wrong; I'm fairly sure it was my name she was screaming last night, not yours. So, it seems like you've already been replaced."

"I will get her back."

"You're welcome to try. I mean, you call yourself an Alpha, but you're acting more like a scared little pup."

"I will end you."

"We'll see who wins in the end."

"Is that all she is to you? A fucking game? You're nothing more than a joke, Gabe. Do you even know how to lead a pack?"

He went to lunge at me, but Thomas held him back. Our instructor then walked in, giving us curious side-eyes before motioning for everyone to take their spots on the mat.

"Today, we'll be sparring in hand-to-hand combat. Do I have any volunteers?"

"I volunteer."

"Big mistake." Said Gabe, standing up, "I also volunteer."

We took our places on the mat, and Professor Payne reiterated the rules we'd both heard a million times.

"No weapons, no shifting. This is hand-to-hand combat. You go until the other one yields or until I say."

Gabe was quick on his feet. If he wasn't so cocky, he might have been unstoppable. I have no idea how long we had been sparring for when he got me into a headlock. His grip was firm, and there was no way I was going to break out of it. I thought I was done. But then he leaned down to whisper in my ear, "Should I tell you how your little mate whines and begs for me to give her my dick, like the good little slut she is?"

His sudden need to provoke me, had him cocking his head back to see my reaction. Big mistake, his grip was still firm, but he was careless. Dropping his guard for only a split-second and that was all I needed. I wrapped my arms around his neck and swung him forward over my back, slamming him over my knee. He released his hold on me, and I stepped into his neck. He couldn't breathe, he couldn't yield, and he would've died as nothing more than the dirt beneath my boot.

"He yields," Professor Payne shouted. I didn't lift my foot; I pressed it down on him harder. "I said he yields!"

I let up, stepped off him, and walked out of class.

Immediately, I pulled my phone out to text Dalton.

(Call a meeting with the Elders. 5 pm.)

It was ten to five when the last member of the council walked in. I greeted Ezra's dad as he walked into my office. "Elder Thorin, thanks for coming," My dad was also there, along with Elder Bear, Elder Smith, and, of course, Zayne. Dalton was also here, but only as my head Gamma.

"Sure thing, Alpha, now what's this all about?"

"First things first, where are we in this investigation against the Storm Cross Pack's Alpha, who has been terrorizing the city?"

"Ah, yes. Well, the low lives have gone into hiding. There have been no new sitings or acts of burglary since they broke into my home and assaulted my daughter."

"They might as well be rogues. They are nothing better than a gang of bandits," Elder Smith chimed in. This was Zayne's Dad. He rarely kept his opinions to himself. He and Zayne were alike in that way.

"Well, keep collaborating with the police, Elder Thorin. Once we find Junior, and we will find him, let me know. He assaulted my mate, and I won't rest until he's found and brought before trial."

"Spoken as a true Alpha," he said with a bow of his head.

"Next on the agenda is the Silver Pack."

"Well, hold on a second there, son. Unless there's been a crime, we do not quarrel with the Silver Pack." My father chimed in.

"We've never "quarreled" with them, Father, because they own half the town with their hotels and business,' but they are

141

steadily growing in strength and power. They could be a serious threat if we don't act now."

"Alpha, sir. The Silver Pack funds our college; without them, we would have no place for our young wolves to learn. I kindly beg you to reconsider," Elder Bear was speaking now.

"I do not intend to wage a war against the members of Silver Pack, but their new Alpha has stolen from me, and I intend to make him alone suffer for his crimes."

"What has he stolen, Alpha?" Elder Smith spoke as though this was of his deepest concern.

"My, mate."

"Son, that's hardly fair. Why don't you just reject her and be on with it? We have plenty of fine wolves for you to choose to mate with."

"Dad, respectfully, shut the fuck up. Ezra is your future, Luna, and I will watch this whole town burn before I let Alpha Gabe have her."

"The Goddess wouldn't have paired them together unless she had a reason for it. I agree with our Alpha. She's to be our future Luna, and Gabe must suffer for crossing that line. He knew damn well what he was doing," said Zayne.

Elder Thorin was now smiling. My Father looked like he was going to tear my head off. Zayne was silently waiting for the Elders to speak. Elder Bear looked like he was going to vomit, and Elder Smith was staring at me intently.

"So, what's the plan?" Elder Smith asked, calling everyone's attention to him. "I mean, you do have a plan. Alpha?"

"Call a meeting with the other pack's Elders. Explain to them that his actions will have repercussions. That we wish for him to be exiled for taking our future Luna. If they should refuse to see reason, make them understand that the peace treaty will be nullified. Alpha Gabe will be exiled for his crimes against Night Tree Pack, or there will be war."

"War? Son, you're speaking nonsense! We haven't had a war in over three hundred years."

"Should they refuse to exile their Alpha, then I will do it for them. Allowing their pack the chance to join ours. Anyone who refuses to bow will be labeled a traitor. Marked as a rogue and forced out of Oakland, so choose your next words carefully, Dad."

"I will support you, son. But I beg you. Please think about what you're about to do."

"Our one true, Alpha," said Elder Thorin, "We knew this day would one day come, John."

"Should we vote?" asked Elder Smith.

"Favor." Said Thorin.

"Favor." Said Smith.

"Favor." Said Zayne, smacking me on the shoulder, to show his support in me.

"Favor." Said Bear.

Everyone turned to look at my father. The vote must be unanimous, or it will be tabled until later.

"Gather the Gamma and tell them to get their squads ready, Dalton, just in case. The next great war might be coming." My Father breathed.

"Dismissed," I said, and all the gentlemen trickled out of my office until it was just my father and me.

"Be careful, Son. The future of our pack is on the line now."

"I don't plan to fail."

"I'm proud of you, Son."

I cleared my throat and sat down at my desk. I had been waiting my whole life to hear those words. It took me declaring war on another pack in our region for them to find their way out of his mouth. But still, the happiness this moment gave me was undeniable. I knew better than to reciprocate my father's tiny mishap in composure.

"Yes, well. It needed to be done." That was all I could manage to say before he, too, was clearing his throat. A glimmer showed in his eyes.

He's proud of me.

CHAPTER SEVENTEEN

JUST FUCKING REJECT ME!

--Ezra's POV

"Ezra, come here, sweetheart; I want you to meet my Beta."

As I walked over to meet Gabe and the other man who was standing there, I got a weird feeling in the pit of my stomach. Gabe and I had been living together for three months, and we barely left the house. I hadn't yet met Beta Thomas or any of his other friends. I went to school and home. I lost my job, not because I wanted to, but because Gabe had all but forced the issue. He said it was putting too much distance between us.

I did agree with him. I was working a lot of hours, but when I asked my boss if she could schedule me for fewer shifts, she wasn't happy. We were short-staffed, and nobody knew this place better than me. I had worked every available hour all summer trying to save for my own Motorcycle, so I'm sure she was also confused by my new request for fewer hours.

That discussion alone wasn't bad until Gabe showed up at my work and demanded she cut my hours. That pissed her off because when I got my schedule, my hours had almost doubled. *A middle finger to my boyfriend,* courtesy of my boss, Nell.

When I got home, he demanded I call and quit. I begged him to just leave it alone, but the next day, while I was at work, he came in.

I was serving a man his coffee, and he gave me a $20 tip. I smiled down at him as I took the tip from his hand. The man patted the top of my hand, saying, "You're very welcome, honey."

If you're anything like me, you'd think there was nothing wrong with that situation, right? Wrong.

Gabe punched him square in the face. I don't think I've ever moved so fast; in seconds, I had managed to move around the counter and firmly place myself between the two men. I was trying to force Gabe away from my customer. It was useless. He was too strong, and my small frame was nothing more than an annoyance to him. A buzzing in his ear, he chose to ignore. Despite my pleas.

"GABE, Stop, what the fuck are you doing!? Get out of here!"

"He touched you!"

"He was thanking me! Have you lost your mind? This is my job! You can't just come here and punch…"

I had said this before, my voice trailed off as Bash's face flashed into my mind. The way he punched Gabe before he threw me over his shoulder and dragged me out, kicking and screaming from Gabe's side. I looked at Gabe, pulling his face into my chest.

"Baby, it was nothing. You need to calm down."

"Ezra, Get him out. Now!" It was Nell; she was beside the older man, holding a fist of napkins to his face that were already soaked through. Crimson red spackled the counter, and the man was screaming in agony. The poor man was still holding his bleeding face in his hands when I looked at Gabe with pleading eyes.

"Oh, don't worry, I'm leaving."

He grabbed my hand and began pulling me to the door. He ripped off my apron and threw it to the counter. "She quits." He yelled to Nell, who was now staring at me with heavy eyes. I have worked there since I was fifteen. My coworkers. Nell. They were like family to me, and now? They were gone in an instant.

Returning home wasn't any better. My own anger, which had bubbled to the surface during our silent car ride home, was spilling over. I couldn't stop myself from speaking, even if every fiber of my being was screaming at me that it was a bad idea.

"You just cost me my Job, Gabe!"

"You're too good for that place, anyway." The silence that had my emotions spiraling into its own mini tornado had inherently affected Gabe, the opposite. He was calm, uncaring, and unbothered by the whole situation.

"That is not your decision to make!"

He moved to my side, his fingers grazing my cheeks as he looked at me. "Kitten, you forget your place."

"My place? What the fuck, Gabe."

"Yes, you are meant to be by my side, Kitten, or have you forgotten?"

"I don't understand, Gabe…This is my life, and I have the right to live it the way I want to."

He sighed. "I'm done talking about this."

I was left standing there, my emotions a disastrous hurricane, whirling through my mind, trying to understand what was going on. He may have been done with this conversation, but I wasn't. I moved after him as he walked away from me, and he turned, looking at me in a way that made it clear he wasn't going to talk to me now. I let him disappear into the bedroom and decided to give him some space, but I still needed answers.

I wanted to know what happened. I still didn't understand why he responded the way he did. Why did he think anything that had happened was okay? But I think, more than anything, I wanted to know how he showed absolutely no remorse for what he had done. Like my feelings didn't even register in his mind. Or worse, they didn't matter.

The next morning, at breakfast, I approached the subject again.

"What happened last night, Gabe?"

"What do you mean?"

I was staring at his face, questioning whether I had lost my mind or if he had lost his. There is no way he doesn't know exactly what I'm talking about.

"I'm going to speak with Nell. Hopefully, she will give me my job back."

"You quit. What's done is done. Let it go."

"I didn't quit, Gabe. You quit for me, and that's the problem."

"Why are you doing this? Can't you just leave it in the past? I already told you I will take care of you. You don't have to work. I can buy you whatever you need."

"I know that, but I want to work. Those people? Nell? they are like my family, and I like my job."

"No." his tone said this was not up for discussion.

"I don't need you to take care of me."

He looked me up and down before getting up from the table and walking away from me. Again. It wasn't necessarily the walking away that broke me. It was the look in his eyes that did it. Like the very look of me was Vile, Repulsive. I felt it down to my core as my body shuddered, crumpling in on itself. Like a skyscraper swaying in an earthquake before it crumbled, leaving nothing but smoke and rubble in its wake.

He wasn't the first person to look at me this way. There was another before him, my dad. I knew how he had felt about me, and I had told myself that it was on him, not me. But after this?

If that were true, how had I somehow managed to show Gabe that same imperfect side of me? The detestable one, the rotten one. Something I never thought this man could make me feel was less than. With him, it was always constant praise, worship, admiration, and longing, yet there I was. Beautifully broken and wishing I had left well enough…alone.

Fast forward a few weeks, and here we are. That day had since faded, but I was realizing just how fragile my heart really was. In nearly four months, I had managed to shatter my heart completely. More broken pieces, to a broken doll, who would never be repaired.

I've been quiet, I've been obedient, I've been everything I thought Gabe wanted me to be. Anything I could do to get us back to where we had been. Now, he was introducing me to his Beta. And I wasn't sure why I had this almost ominous feeling about it. I wanted this. It felt like we were "us" again. He was happy. So then, why did the sight of his Beta send an unsettling chill down my spine, causing the baby hairs on the back of my neck to stand up?

The atmosphere surrounding that man just felt off, but I went to Gabe, allowing him to pull me into his side as I smiled at the very buff, very scary man standing in front of me. It was clear he spent a decent amount of time in the gym. Every part of his body was perfectly chiseled. He was tall. Maybe the tallest man I've ever seen.

"Ezra, this is Thomas. Thomas, meet my girl, Ezra."

"Hello Thomas, it's great to meet you."

"I've heard a lot about you, Ezra. I hope you've been taking good care of my Alpha here."

"I do my best."

"I was just telling your boyfriend here that I was having a party tonight. Can I count on you two to be there?"

"Of course we will be, man," Gabe answered for the both of us. And I smiled at Thomas again.

"Can't wait."

It's no secret to anyone who truly knows me that I don't care for parties. This wasn't something I was excited about, but then...

"Gabe? Can I go shopping with Kit? She could help me pick out a nice outfit for the party tonight, and I really want to look good for you. Please?"

He was silent as he looked at me no doubt debating whether or not this was allowable. It hurt that he had that power over me. But when he spoke, the excitement drowned out the doubt in my heart.

"Go ahead and buy yourself something sexy," he said, passing me his debit card with a playful wink, "The pin is your birthday. Treat yourself to whatever catches your eye."

I was beaming. I hadn't been able to see Kit in a few weeks, and I missed her. "Thank you!" I kissed his cheek, and he smacked my ass as I wiggled off to call Kit.

Maybe there was nothing going on here, and I was just in my own head for no reason. Thankfully, Kit picked up after the first ring. I was so excited to spend time with her, and I didn't know if she was busy or not.

"Kit!"

"Ezra, what the fuck, bitch. You cannot just ghost me like this. I have been so worried about you! Haven't you been getting my texts?"

"I know, I know. I'm sorry. I miss you too. I've been meaning to message you back. I've just been so busy. I was hoping you might want to hang out later, though. I need your help! There is this party tonight with Gabe's Beta, and I need to buy something to wear. What do you say to, some dinner and light shopping?"

"Just us girls?"

"Yes, just us girls."

"Of course, I'll go shopping with you, Ezzie. I'll meet you at my house around 4?"

"See you then, love you, Kit!"

"I love you too, Ezzie."

When I hung up the phone, I looked up to see Bash standing five feet in front of me with Zayne. I wasn't allowed to speak to him, though. Gabe didn't want me to talk to him, and out of respect for our relationship, I did everything I could to avoid him. I was so distracted by my call with Kit that I didn't even notice I had been walking straight toward him until it was too late.

"Ez." the way he said my name made my heart flutter. He was the only one who ever called me Ez. I missed him, even if I wasn't supposed to. He was one of my closest friends, and he was also still my mate, so avoiding him forever was never going to happen, no matter how hard I tried.

He was moving toward me well before my mind caught up with his movements, and it was too late to run away.

"Hey, Bash."

"Hey, it's so good to see you, and without Gabe?"

"He's…busy with Thomas right now."

"Lucky me." He said, tucking his hands into his jean pockets. God, he looked so good. I missed the sight of him, his boyish grin, his tousled hair, his… *No. No. Stop!*

"So, how have you been?" I asked, but I could literally feel myself shrinking before him as I stared up into those brown eyes. I wasn't sure why I thought this situation called for making small talk, but he saw right through me and skipped to what really mattered.

"You know the answer to that question already, Ez. I miss you. Nothing is right anymore. Not without you."

"I didn't want to hurt you, Bash. I mean, I never meant to. I just…"

"You're my mate, Ez. We are meant to be together. I'm sure you feel that. You must." He grabbed my hand, but I pulled it back, holding it at my chest.

"I love Gabe." My tone was supposed to be more resolute, but from the look now on his face, I could tell even he didn't believe those words.

"Do you?"

"Yes, I do. I told you I couldn't be what you needed me to be, Bash."

"I just needed you to be you, Ez." He reached for my hands again, and I stepped back.

"I can't do this," I said, shaking my head, trying to side-step him.

"Please, Ez? Talk to me." He said stepping in front of me again, "You were meant to be with me. It's supposed to be us. The Goddess..."

"The Goddess was wrong."

"The Goddess is never wrong."

This was getting us nowhere. I swung my backpack, which was sliding down my arm now, back up over my shoulder, "This time, she was Bash. I need you to let me go. Please."

"I'll never let go. Not if there's hope. I can't; you're my mate." He was moving closer to me, trying to regain the distance I had put between us.

"Then just fucking REJECT ME!" I couldn't stop the words from escaping; I had been avoiding this...because, despite everything, I cared about him.

He and I both knew that I couldn't reject him. He was an alpha, and I was his fated mate. Which meant his rejection could kill me if I weren't mated to another. But did I want to be mated to Gabe? I mean...*did I?*

The look in his eyes was familiar. It was the same look I hid from the world my whole life—the look that begged the question, "Why am I not good enough? Why won't you just love me?"

I've spent my whole life on the questioning side of love. But here I am, forcing the same pain onto him. Bash, of all people. Who has always been there, my loyal and dependable friend?

"FUCK, Ez! Why are you so goddamned stubborn?!"

He leaned down and kissed me.

Fire was radiating through me. The same fire I had felt the first time we kissed. His kiss held all the words he'd never spoken. Four words, to be exact. *Because I love you.*

CHAPTER EIGHTEEN

"PLAN B"

I pushed Bash away from me. Just in time to see Gabe sprinting toward us. His eyes held that same darkness I was beginning to expect from him. Those were the eyes that caused my insides to twist and knot until I was forcing the bile back down into my stomach.

"You forget your place again, Kitten?" he asked, grabbing my arm and pulling me away from Bash. It hurt, but I was frozen.

When I tried to speak, I couldn't find my voice. My insides had completely turned on me, and the only sound that managed to escape my lips was a barely audible squeak. This time, there was no one to curse other than my own stupid heart or whatever was left of it.

"Touch her again, and I will end you, Bingham." He turned his fury onto Bash. Who held that same calm, collected demeanor he usually conveyed. But refused to even acknowledge Gabe's presence. He looked at me. Only at me. And all I could see was torment and anguish.

"Let's go," Gabe pulled me off beside him. It was forceful. And I pleaded against his grip on my arm.

"Gabe, you're hurting me. Let go."

His hand relaxed on my arm, but he didn't let go. "I leave you alone for five minutes, and you're making out with your ex? Have you lost your damn mind?!"

"I wasn't making out with my ex, Gabe. I ran into him; it's not like I sought him out. And I asked him to reject me."

This made him happy because his eyes softened the way they would when I was being a good girl or when he was feeling pleased. But we were still next to Bash, who was watching the whole interaction.

"I suggest you get your hands off of her." He said firmly.

"This doesn't concern you, Bingham. If it weren't for the treaty, you'd already be dead."

"And if Professor Payne hadn't saved your ass, you'd already be dead. That treaty means nothing to me. But your hands on Ezra, now that means a great deal."

"She's made her choice, Bingham. Except it or don't, but either way, she's leaving with me."

"Stop!" I had heard enough.

Both men looked at me then. For once, my big girl voice was working. But now that both men were looking at me, I needed to choose my next words carefully.

"Bash, please just go. You've done enough damage here for one day, don't you think?" His gaze fell from mine, but not before I caught a glimpse of the pain flickering in his eyes as if a deep wound had been momentarily exposed. That had hurt him. Which I could live with if it meant the two men before me, the only two men I had ever dared to care for, would stop fighting.

"And Gabe, I chose you. But I can speak for myself. Now, we are all going to be late for class, so can you please walk me there?"

I was looking at Gabe now, and he bent down, threading his fingers in mine. As we walked off, I peeked over my shoulder. Bash was still standing there, still watching me. I forced my eyes toward Gabe.

"Hey, you know I love you, right?"

"I know. I just hate that guy."

I don't think I heard a single word that Professor Marc's said during that class. I was so anxious about which Gabe was going to be waiting for me outside after class. Because I was beginning to realize there were two sides to this man. The incredibly sweet, caring, and loving one who looked at me like I was the Goddess' gift to this world. The one that I had fallen for. Then there was the one that had my leg bouncing a million miles a minute, my heart beating at an insane rate, the one that looked at me like I was Vile.

After class was over, Gabe was leaning against the wall in his usual spot. My pace slowed as I approached him. When his eyes locked onto mine, that irresistible grin lit up his face, radiating confidence and charm that made everything else around us fade away. The weight in my heart evaporated as I ran to him, and he held his arms out to me, wrapping me in his loving embrace. He had cooled off, and I was happy to find him in a better mood.

"Ready, Kitten?"

"Yes, please!"

He kissed me then and gripped my ass, pulling me up into his arms; a playful squeal escaping my lips was reciprocated with a low, hungry growl from his. I wrapped my legs around him and let him carry me to the car.

"There's my good girl."

"Gabe? I'm meeting Kit at four."

"Maybe you should just cancel, Kitten."

"What? I already told her I'd meet her. I can't just not go."

When we got to the house, he walked around to my door and picked me up, carrying me inside.

"We'll see. I think I'll just keep you home tonight, all to myself."

"Please, I want to go. You already said I could go," I begged and pouted at him with my eyes. I didn't want to go to the party, but I was really looking forward to some girl time with Kit.

"Show me, Kitten." He said as we entered the house. He kicked the door shut behind us and let me down in front of him. He tossed his keys on the side table and pushed me down by my shoulders so that I was kneeling in front of him. "Show me how badly you want to go." It wasn't a question. And I obeyed.

As I released his already-hardened cock from his pants, he smiled down at me, "That's right, Kitten. Suck Daddy's cock. It's been throbbing all day, waiting for you."

Then he grabbed my hair and pinched my nose, thrusting his cock deep into my throat with so much force that I gagged, and tears formed in my eyes. He wanted to hurt me. He was pissed, and this was my punishment.

"Do you like the way I fuck that dirty Slut mouth of yours?" he asked. I couldn't breathe. I was seconds away from passing out when he released my nose and pulled his cock out.

"Yes," I said, trying to catch my breath. He needed this, and I was going to give it to him. Whether I wanted to or not.

I reached up, pinching his balls and massaging them gently between my fingertips while he fucked my mouth, still firmly gripping my hair. He tilted his head back, moaning louder and louder as he thrust deep into my mouth. While my sobs and whimpers grew louder.

"Yes, warm-up where all your babies live…show them some love, swallow them, gargle them…then let me drop them in your pussy."

He pulled out and shoved his balls into my mouth, and I swirled them around in my mouth.

"Good girl, does that pussy need some attention, Kitten? Is it dripping down your thighs?"

Fuck no. It wasn't. Not that it mattered.

My refusal to speak irritated him, and I screamed as he flipped me around, pushing my face into the wall. He was already pulling down my pants before I even got my hands up to help brace myself against the wall. He gave my ass a hard slap as he grabbed my hips and buried himself deep into my pussy.

He wasn't wasting any more time; he pounded my pussy until it was soaked; even after I came, he continued to thrust. Until he felt his own sweet release.

"Fucking slut." He said, pulling me up by my throat and kissing my mouth.

"You didn't...pull out." I breathed.

"Why would I?" he said, looking down at me, with disgust.

"It's just, you haven't before... and I'm not on birth control."

"Well then, let's hope my sperm do their job so I can keep one as a pet."

I was still floating somewhere far above Oakland, from the insane pleasure that had just melted out of me, despite the brutality of it. I was also angry with him all over again. And this made me realize just how messed up we were. *Toxic.* This love and hate that I was feeling was Toxic. He didn't think to talk to me before deciding I would be having his babies, because it didn't matter. Fighting with him about it would only cause more harm, though, so I kissed him again before picking up my clothes.

"I'm going to get a shower, Daddy."

"No."

"What?"

"No shower today, Kitten."

"But...you just."

"Put my baby in you? Let's hope so, Kitten. Now have fun before I change my mind."

"You want me pregnant?!"

"You think he'll still want you when you're having our baby? If he doesn't want to release you from that bond, I'll give him no choice."

"You're doing this…to force Bash to reject me?"

"Kitten, Go. Or stay. But either way, you aren't getting a shower."

I slipped my pants back on and went to leave. There was zero chance of fixing this if I was still here with him, and I wasn't ready to think about young pups running around.

"You heard what I said, Kitten?"

"Yes, Daddy. No shower. Got it."

When I got to Kit's, I went inside and to my room. Technically, I still paid rent here, or rather, Gabe did. So, this was still my room. I grabbed some clothes and went to the bathroom. Kit walked in and took one look at me, then wrapped her arms around me.

"Ezzie, what happened? Shhh…it's okay honey…it's okay."

"Kit, nothing is okay. Nothing. I can't…breathe," I was sobbing uncontrollably. Kit reached up into the shower and turned on the water for me.

"Did he hurt you?" she was turning me and looking for the bruises. But Gabe wasn't my dad, his bruises weren't on my body, they were on my heart.

I shook my head no.

"Kit, he wants to have a baby."

"What?! That's insane. Ezzie, you're only eighteen. You two just started dating. That's ridiculous. You can't have his baby."

"I know that, Kit." The pure sarcasm that filtered out in my tone was undeniably sharp, cutting through the conversation like a knife. Kit took a step back, folding her arms in front of her chest.

"So, you two got into a fight?"

"No. He…just decided, and he didn't pull out."

"Ezra Isabelle Kent. Get your ass in there, now," She pointed into the shower, and I knew she was pissed. I just didn't know if she was pissed at me or Gabe. Probably both. And I couldn't blame her either way.

"I'll go to the store and buy a plan B. Now clean yourself up."

"Okay. And Kit. I missed you."

"I missed you too, Ezzie. You aren't going back there."

"I love him, Kit."

"Maybe, but you still aren't going back there."

Before I could argue with her further, she was gone. I took the moment to look into the mirror at myself. I was ghostly white, except for the bloodshot eyes that screamed back at me from my own reflection. I pulled my shirt up, running my fingers over my stomach like Gabe used to do. What if I did get pregnant? What would happen then? Would my baby have a good life? It wasn't always like this. When things were good…they were so good.

"She's right. Don't go back."

"Lana?" I was shocked by the sudden voice that dared speak to me after abandoning me for months.

"It isn't love. No one who loved you would cause you so much pain."

"What do you know about love? You left me! Just like everyone else, and you promised. Lana, you promised you'd never leave."

"I'm still here, Ezra."

"Where were you?"

"Waiting."

I scoff. "Waiting? For what?"

"For you to be ready. For you to see the truth."

"What truth? Lana? I don't know what to do," I cried again.

"Yes, you do. The truth is that love and ownership…aren't the same thing."

"This is about Kane?"

"No. This is about you. Do you not think you deserve better? When you ask yourself, who has truly been there for you, is it Gabe's face you see?"

My shoulders slumped forward, my face falling freely into my hands, and a flood of emotions threatened my very existence as my brain shut down completely. I felt like I'd forgotten how to even breathe, the basic rhythm of life was just slipping away. The weight of my sorrow pressed down on my chest with terrifying might, and my heart ached with the intensity of it all. *How has air itself turned against me?*

"No. It's. Not. Gabe."

CHAPTER NINETEEN

SHOULD I FALL…

I wasn't sure how long I had been crying in the shower when I finally turned off the now icy-cold water. My body trembled from the heat of the air when I finally stepped out. Goosebumps forming on my arms. My heart was finally beating at a pace that made sense, steady and calm. When I finally exited the bathroom, it was Beth sitting outside of the door.

"Are you okay?" she asked, looking at me with something other than hatred in her eyes. Something even worse, sympathy. *She fucking felt sorry for me.*

"Do you care?" I asked, raising a brow.

"About you? Not particularly, but nobody deserves that, not even you. Look, I know I've been a Bitch; can I explain? You don't even need to talk. Just sit and listen."

I moved to the couch and nodded my head at her. Anything was better than the inner dialogue I had running rampant inside my own head. She sat beside me, she talked, and I listened. For the most part.

"I've spent my whole life with Bash. I always thought it would be me and him," she began. "You've got to believe me when I say that I didn't understand the magnitude of his feelings for you. You took him away from me. And I hated you for it, but I know now, Ezra. It isn't the bond that changed Bash. It was you. Even with you completely out of the picture, it's you for him. It's always been."

"I know."

"Then why? Why are you making him suffer without you."

"I'm not, Beth." There was nothing left of me. It was my voice, and I barely recognized the sound. There was nothing left of who I used to be. "I asked him to reject me. He won't let me go."

"Because he fucking loves you." She was standing over me now. I looked up at her, but I didn't feel anything. I was numb.

"It doesn't matter."

"How can you say that? How can you be so heartless?"

"You wouldn't understand."

"Fucking. Try. Me." The words were broken; she was back to angry. Which was a much better look on her. The only thing worse than feeling sorry for yourself was watching people who would never understand look at you and think they knew the special kind of fucked up you really were.

"I would never be good enough for him, Beth. I can't be his Luna. I can't fix anyone; I can't even fix myself."

"That's the dumbest thing you've ever fucking said."

"Yeah, well, I'm feeling especially dumb today, or haven't you heard?"

"Oh, I heard. But…" She got down on my level so our eyes were parallel, and then she continued.

"When are you going to look around and realize? Even with everything you've been through, you're sitting here in front of me. So what? You're a little broken. We all have scars, Ezra. Who cares if yours cut deeper? Don't you realize that's what makes you so powerful? You're stronger than the rest of us."

"I'm not strong, Beth. I'm a coward."

"Yeah, well. Right now, you're acting like one, but that isn't who you are. So, get off your ass and fucking change it."

Kit stepped in through the front door and looked from Beth to me and back to Beth before asking, "What did you fucking say to her?"

She stood up and said, "Only the truth," before flipping her hair over her shoulder and prancing, yes fucking prancing, out of the room. Maybe there were some skipping movements there, either way. I burst out laughing. Kit was staring at me like I had just jumped off Fort Pitt Bridge and completely lost my mind. Perhaps I did, but at that moment, I appreciated that snarky little she-wolf.

My laughter was cut short, though, when Bash strode through the door. His hair was flowy, his jacket glistening from the sunlight outside the door, and his eyes...just his eyes—were dangerously deep, brown. And I choked on my laugh, banging on my chest and then turning my eyes on Kit. Who threw me a Pharmacy bag, which I just barely caught, before she smiled and walked back out the door.

"Is it okay that I'm here?" Bash asked, taking only one step into the room.

"I could use a friend," I responded. And he walked in and pulled me into his lap, cradling me in his arms. I let him. Because right now, as selfish as it was. I needed this. *I needed him.*

--Bash's POV

"What did we hear from the Silver Pack elders?" I looked at the five men spread out before me.

"They choose to stand with their Alpha." Said Smith.

"Then their graves have already been dug unless their Alpha chooses to settle this, traditionally. Send correspondence to Silver Pack that I formally challenge Alpha Gabe. Should I fall..."

"Zero chance, Sebastian." Said my father, cutting me off.

"Should I fall, I expect you to step up in my place, Zayne. Keep our pack unified. We're bigger and stronger than Silver Pack. But if chaos ensues, many lives will be lost, so protect them."

I was looking at Zayne, and I didn't even need to say the words. He knew me better than I knew myself. "I will protect Ezra with my life." He assured me.

I mouthed the words "*thank you*" to him and turned to Elder Thorin, "They've captured Alpha Junior?"

"Yes," he nodded, "I received correspondence this morning from the officers under our authority. He's currently being held at Alleghany County Jail."

"Arrange a time for questioning." I ordered.

"Yes, Alpha."

"Thank you, dismissed." I waved the men off. And grabbed my motorcycle helmet.

"Son, is now really the right time for a stroll around town?"

"Now might be all I've got, and I plan to make every minute count," I said, strolling out of the room.

When I got to Ezra's, I looked up at the house and it almost felt like the last few months had never happened. Like Ezra hadn't disappeared from my life completely, stealing my heart away with her. The grass was still overgrown because these girls suck at lawn care. I would have to make it a point to mow that before the end of the week.

The flag that hung to the left of the door still swayed in the breeze. The cement walk, where I watched Ezra sprint away from me after that first ride with her, was now littered with leaves but otherwise left unchanged. I thought back to that day; it was the most amusingly awkward moment of my life, but I couldn't help but laugh every time I thought about it. I also couldn't help but remember how good Ezra's ass looked as she strode away from me.

Everything was exactly as it had been before us and will no doubt be the same after us. I pulled out my phone and sent Ezra a message.

(I'm outside. Ready?)

(Be out in a minute.)

As I waited, my mind began to wander. I had no idea if I was strong enough to take on Gabe. But I knew that I couldn't just sit by and do nothing, either. I promised Ez I would burn this whole town to the ground before I let any man put another finger on her. I failed her with that once, and I refused to fail her a second time. Gabe would pay for everything, and he would pay with his very life. Challenging Gabe, Alpha to Alpha, could save so many lives. Possibly end the war before it began. Only one life needed to be lost. His.

My hands bore into the handles of my motorcycle, white-knuckled when I saw Ezra slipping out of the door, turning, and locking it behind her.

She looked happier and healthier than I had seen her in months. I couldn't help but smile at how beautiful she was. And the smile she flashed back at me was so genuine. She was rubbing her hands together and blowing into her palms as she made her way to my side.

The air had chilled, the leaves had begun to fall, and the entire world was shifting, getting ready for the cool winter to arrive. And I wondered what kind of memories those winter months would bring if I survived. Goddess, I wanted to live for this woman.

"Shit, it's fucking cold." She said as she approached me.

"Yeah, you might need this." I lifted a box out of my backpack and handed it to her. She looked at it questionably before accepting it and pulling on the ribbon that held it together. The look on her face as she opened the box, lifting the leather jacket out, was well worth the awkward ride here. The box was too big to fit entirely in my bag, so I had to hold the damned thing in place. It made for an interesting ride and managed to attract some rather comical expressions from the people I'd passed.

"Bash, this is a fucking masterpiece!" she was now holding the heavy leather bike jacket against her chest, hugging it tightly, and I remembered what it felt like to be that close. The softness of her skin, the sweetness of her scent, something I could never really distinguish but was uniquely satisfying to my senses. I longed to be that close to her again, but I will never complain again about being in the friend zone. Even if she were so much more than that to me, I would wait this time for her to be ready. And if I die before ever being able to claim this woman.

Nope. Not going there. *I will not die*; I will live to see that day. I will live to see the day I can call her mine.

"You can't own a motorcycle without first owning an equally badass biker jacket."

"I don't know what I did to deserve you, Bash."

Tears were forming in the edges of her eyes, those dangerously soul-catching baby blue eyes.

"Come on, Babygirl. Let's get you your bike."

As she zipped up the jacket, she spun before folding her hands and legs in front of her, shrugging her shoulders. It should have looked awkward, but it didn't. It just looked like her, the Ez I had fallen for all those months ago before I even had time to register it.

Ez meant more to me than any other person on this earth. Not because the Goddess handpicked her for me but because she was the one who saw me for who I really was, beneath the title. She was my anchor in the storm, the one who made me believe in love. Because of her, I was a stronger, better leader, and I believed in the possibility of a brighter tomorrow.

"Soo? What do you think?" she asked, nearly falling from the uncoordinated position she had somehow locked herself into.

As my hands reached out to steady her, the words forced their way out, "I think I love you."

"You think you love me?"

"No," I quickly corrected, "I know I love you, Ez."

My status—the same status I still held—would soon be put to the test in honor of the beautifully awkward yet unfathomable beauty that was Ezra. But I knew it was also the reason why she was not already by my side. There was something holding her back, and I needed to know what it was.

"I know we're just friends, Ez. I just needed you to hear it. At least once, I needed to say it out loud. I love you."

"Bash, I…"

I braced myself for the inevitable fallout of the words I dared to say. She sighed, then lifted my face in her hands. Those wonderfully soft, warm, breath-kissed hands. And then she pulled my lips to hers.

She kissed me.

She kissed me, and I leaned into that kiss like it was the only thing keeping me tethered to this world. All the tension and fear melted away in that moment. Her kiss was everything I needed, and I felt like I could finally breathe again. It was like finding my way home after being lost for so long.

When I finally released my hold on Bash, he looked at me like he was searching for some type of reassurance, some sign that the moment we had just shared was real. My eyes softened as the warmth in my heart rose to my face.

"I know I love you, too. And I'm also so sorry it took me this long to say it."

His eyes reflected the relief his wolf was feeling, and his body showed it. I watched every muscle in his perfectly sculpted body relax. And then he pulled me into him. It was like everything wrong in the world had somehow managed to change courses at that moment.

"This is real, isn't it? You love me too, Ez? If it's a dream, don't wake me up."

"I already said it once. You're going to make me repeat it?" I chuckled, bringing my hands to his chest, before reaching up to "Boop" his nose.

"I don't think you could ever say it enough times for me to believe them."

"Well, believe it, Sebastian Lee Bingham, I love you. I think I always have, and I'm done denying it."

His lips on my forehead before he leaned his against mine...spoke as much as every intimate moment that had ever passed between us.

We were locked in that moment, inhaling, and exhaling the same breaths, for only moments when his jaw tensed, and when he pulled away from me, he looked like he was in pain. My hands were moving before I could even think, trying to force his gaze back to mine. I needed that reassurance now. Was it too late? Did I lose him and not even know it?

"Bash? What's wrong?"

He was in pain. He could never hide that away, although he tried. "Talk to me…"

"I just got you, Ez. I can't lose you now."

"Hey, I'm here. I want you, Bash. I love you."

"I love you too." His hand was moving through his hair; something was making him nervous, and that was his tell.

"Tell me." When he looked at me, I realized it wasn't pain he was feeling. It was panic.

"Bash? Talk to me, please." I pleaded. Something was wrong. He was keeping something from me. He'd never kept anything from me before. So, whatever was causing this, was seriously bad.

"We should get your bike, Ez. We'll run out of time; we can talk about this later."

"Fuck the bike, let's talk about this now." I was getting mad now, what was he hiding, and why? I pulled away from him slightly. "Tell me what's going on, Bash."

He sighed, "We're on the brink of a war between our packs, Ez. And I," he paused, searching for any words that would help soften the blow, but he obviously couldn't find them.

“I issued a challenge to Gabe.” He finished.

“You challenged Gabe?! Are you fucking kidding me?!”

“It needed to be done, Ez. Either we settle it this way, or our people suffer. We tried to speak with their Elders, and the situation escalated. I didn’t see another way.”

“YOU COULD DIE!”

“I won’t.”

“You don’t know that, Bash. Gabe is…you aren’t the same.” I placed my hand over his heart, “Your heart is going to kill you, Bash, because I assure you; he doesn’t have one.”

“Loving you doesn’t make me weak, Ez. It makes me stronger.”

“You’re a damned fool if you believe that. Oh God, Bash what have you done?”

“Ez, I’m going to win. I have to. We’ve come too far to lose us now, so I have to win, and I will.”

CHAPTER TWENTY

UNRAVELING TRUTHS

"Zayne, hey. Bash isn't answering his phone, and I'm…well, do you know where he is?" I asked into the phone.

"Yes."

"Great." I said, relieved, but when he didn't say anything, I asked, "So, are you going to tell me where that is?"

"No."

What in the actual fuck does he mean, no?

"Quit being such a Beta and tell me where he is, Zayne!"

"He's fine, Ezra. The challenge isn't until Saturday. It's just urgent pack business. I promise he's fine."

"You're really pissing me off." I retorted.

"Yeah, that's kind of my job, as Beta."

"Well, I also really fucking hate you."

"Yeah, I get that a lot too, actually. But while I have you on the phone…I was hoping I could talk to you about something concerning Bash."

"Okay? So, talk."

"I don't mean to push…but I want Bash to have the best possible chance at winning…"

"Me, too."

"He's going to lose, Ezra. Your bond makes him weak."

"Fuck! I KNOW. He won't listen to me." I was pacing now. Thinking it was one thing, but hearing Zayne mimic my thoughts, this was bad—really bad.

"We need to stop this, Zayne. Tell me you have a plan."

"I do. But it's not what you think."

There was another long pause. A pause that felt never-ending as my mind began racing. A million thoughts of what Zayne could mean, a million thoughts that weren't helpful in the least. I already knew the answer that tipped my tongue. The words, like acid, I couldn't bear to speak myself. Take me out of this equation, and Bash would have a chance. I waited anxiously, my foot taking on a life of its own as it began tapping incessantly. Irritation laced with sadness erupted from within as I turned my serpent tongue on Zayne.

"Well, if you would just speak. Instead of talking in circles, I would be able to understand what the fuck it is that you're trying to say!"

"Your bond only makes him weak because he hasn't claimed you yet."

Another deafening pause as he waited for me to process his words. He didn't want me to walk away from the bond. He wanted me to accept it.

"You want me to mate with him?"

"If you fully mate, then he will be strong enough to win, Ezra. A mated Alpha, especially one with a fated bond, would easily best an unmated Alpha. I know you don't want to be our Luna, but is that worth his life?"

"It was never about what I wanted, Zayne. It's always been about what was best for our pack, for Bash."

"Then mate with him, Ezra. He won't do it unless you make it clear it's what you want. He won't risk losing you again, even if it costs him his life. So, make him mark you. Please. Ezra, he's more than my Alpha. He's my best friend."

This conversation was going downhill fast. I didn't want to lose Bash, but I wasn't sure I could be their Luna either. My mind was spinning. It's been two days since I told Bash I loved him. Two days and the only thing I knew for sure was that no matter what, Bash was going to follow this through.

"I don't want to lose him either, Zayne. I love him."

"He's at the prison. They caught that no good piece of shit that hurt you, Alpha Junior Black."

"What?"

"They finally caught that no good…"

"No, I fucking heard you; you said, Junior Black? He's the Alpha of Storm Cross Pack?"

"Yeah?"

"And he's in custody? And Bash is with him now?"

"Yes, he wants him brought to trial for what he did to you."

My temple felt like it was going to pound right out of my head. How did I not know any of this?

"Because you were in Gabe's Prison."

"It wasn't a prison, Lana."

"Could have fooled me."

"Okay, I know that sucked for you. I'm sorry."

"Not only for me."

"Point made; now, can we move on? And will you stay out of my thoughts, please?"

"Have you ever been inside your mind? It's exhausting."

"I need to think."

"Please don't."

She was laughing as I pushed her out of my mind. For an Alpha, an accusation like that was a death sentence. One little mistruth that gained me my freedom was going to ruin his life. And I still had so many questions. Questions only he had the answers to. But if I told the truth…my dad would surely deny it. Still, I couldn't just sit here and do nothing.

"He didn't hurt me, Zayne." Telling lies was easy. Telling the truth? This was going to be painful. Unraveling truths could do just as much damage.

"I don't understand, Ezra. We've been searching for Junior for months… he and his bandits were the ones who broke into your house. Bash has been tearing this city apart to find him."

"He didn't hurt me, Zayne."

"You just don't remember anything. I promise this is the guy."

"I remember everything, Zayne, and it wasn't Junior."

"What?"

"I have to get to the prison,"

"Ezra? I don't under…"

I didn't even bother listening to his words…I had to get to the prison and fast. For the first time since I had gotten my wolf, I shifted.

"Get us there now," I told Lana.

"About damn time," she snarled as she took off.

--Bash's POV

As I was sitting, waiting for the officers to bring in Junior, the main door flung open, "Ma'am, you can't go in there!" said one of the officers as Ezra strode into the room.

"Fucking watch me," she told him as she walked in. Her hands perched on those succulent hips, causing me to grin. She was so much different now from when I had met her. Stronger, and it only made her more irresistible to me.

"It's fine, Carter. She's with me."

She turned her head and gave the officer a cocky "I told you so" smile, and I rose to meet her.

"How did you know I was here, Ez?"

But I didn't wait for her to answer. I pulled her into my arms before sucking that luscious bottom lip into my mouth. "Fuck, you taste so good."

The corners of her lips turned up as she placed her hands against my chest as she often did. Leaning back slightly, pulling her lips away so that she could look at me.

"First," she said.

Nope. Not done yet.

She was so close that her scent assaulted my nose as I breathed her in. I placed my hand at the nape of her neck and pulled her back into the kiss. There wasn't enough time, and I wasn't going to waste a minute of it. She pulled away again, placing her soft fingers against my lips as I exhaled deeply.

"This is not the time or the place, Bash." She chuckled, "And second, this is important. I need to talk to you about Junior."

"You weren't supposed to be here, Ez," I said with a mischievous smile. "But since you are, I'd rather talk about the correct time and place so I can get back to kissing you."

"Yeah? Funny how you keep doing all this shit, in my name, without even filling me in on it."

It was clear she wasn't going to let me kiss her again. I reached up to cup her face softly.

"Don't be mad; I just didn't want you to have to face him after what he'd done to you."

"Junior would never hurt me."

My head cocked to the side at her tone, "You sound so sure, but I read the report, Ez. I saw the damage firsthand; you didn't even see the man that attacked you."

"Okay, so that might not be…entirely accurate."

I took a step back, leaning against the table in the center of the room, my hands folding in front of my chest.

"No?"

"I know who attacked me…and it wasn't Junior, but he is hiding something, and I need to know what it is."

"What?" I wasn't sure I even heard her correctly. "Who attacked you?"

She began pacing, her fingers busying themselves at her sides. She was still keeping secrets. Still refusing to let me in.

"Ez." My voice trembled, betraying the frustration and desperate hope I had felt just days ago when she admitted her feelings for me. "Please, just tell me what's going on."

She stopped pacing, her eyes darting all around as if she were searching for the right words. When she finally looked at me, her expression was torn between fear and resolve.

"I can't," she whispers, her voice barely audible.

I stepped closer to her like I was trying to bridge the emotional gap between us yet again. "Ez, I love you. Whatever it is, we can face it together."

She hesitated, her fingers clenching and unclenching at her sides. There was that internal battle again. The one she had fought the first day we spent together. She wouldn't let me in then, but so much has changed between then and now. As I locked my fingers in hers, everything fell into the silence around us. The room was charged with so many unspoken words and hidden fears. We were both standing on the precipice of something that could change everything if only she would let me in.

"Can you please just trust me?" she begged.

"I don't know, Ez. Why don't you explain what you mean because right now?" I lowered my voice so that only she could hear me. "Right now, it kind of sounds like you lied to a police officer and to me."

"I never lied to you, Bash. I just didn't tell you everything either."

All those secrets were a sign. She was hiding something because she didn't think she could trust me either, or worse, she didn't really love me.

My voice wavered as I asked the hardest question of my life to the only person who could entirely break me and my wolf. She had my heart entirely; she had to know that she held all the power here. There was nothing I wouldn't do in her name, no fight I wouldn't face, to keep her safe.

"Ez, I need to know…do you still love me? Because right now, it feels like you're pushing me away again."

She looked at me, her eyes wide with surprise and pain. "Of course I love you," she responded, but her voice was breaking now. "But this isn't about us. It's about keeping you and our pack safe."

The doubt that hung in the air made our entire relationship seem fragile and uncertain. This whole time, I thought I was protecting her, and she was suffering in silence. She was trying to protect me, but from what? Was that what the last few months were with Gabe?

"You've got about 5 minutes to tell me something now, Ez, because Alpha Black will be coming through those doors." I pointed to the inmate's access door but never took my eyes off hers. "And he's either going to confess, or I'll force his confession out of him."

She was shaking her head now. "I need to talk to him, Bash."

"Never going to fucking happen."

"There isn't enough time. I need you to trust me. Bash, I need to talk to him."

"This is an open investigation; I can't just allow…"

"As Alpha, I'm sure you can allow a victim to address the accused…in her own case."

"Don't…Ez, don't do that."

"Then don't make me do that!"

If I didn't love this woman, this would have been a simple request, and I hated that she was right. As her Alpha, I could do this.

But as the man, desperately in love with her. I felt an intense need to protect what was mine.

"You are the man I love more than anything else. But you are also my Alpha."

It was like she could see into my soul. She knew exactly what I was feeling.

"If you can't do this because you love me or because you trust me. Do this because you know, as my Alpha, you owe me this right."

"I just want to protect you, Ez."

"I am not the same girl I was last year, Bash. I don't need you to protect me. I need you to trust me. I promise I'll tell you everything you want to know, but that man is the only one standing between me and the answers I've been looking for my whole life…I need this."

Two things were absolute now. She held all the power in this relationship, and I was not going to win this argument. "Fine. But I stay with you."

Her eyes softened, her lips reaching up to meet mine. She was right; she was not the same shy, awkward girl I had fallen in love with. She could hold her own against her Alpha because she was my Luna. If we weren't still sitting in this room, awaiting Alpha Black, I would've marked her then and there.

Goddess, *she was magnificent.*

CHAPTER TWENTY-ONE

LITTLE TOY.

--Ezra's POV

The door opened, and the second Junior saw me, his expression shifted from anger to pure amusement.

"Well, if it isn't my favorite little toy, is it playtime?" he asked as the officer secured his cuffs to the opposite side of the large, steel table where Bash and I were currently sat.

Bash let out a deep snarl next to me, and my hand instinctively rested against his thigh. When he felt my touch, his body relaxed slightly, but his gaze held firm.

I watched as Juno leaned forward, sending me a wink, as a mischievous grin spread across his face. "Always so good to see you, Juno."

"Wish I could say the same, Little Toy. But I have no choice here."

"Seems you don't," I said, my voice calm, unwavering.

"Well, enough of the pleasantries, then. What is it you want from me," He ignored Bash's hot gaze and looked straight at me, studying my face.

"I want answers."

"Awe, so we're back to this then, are we?" he leaned back into the chair as far as his secured hands would allow, "And here I thought, you just missed our time together." He was trying to provoke Bash, and up until now, Bash's narrowed gaze had not wavered. His eyes locked on Juno, filled with fierce determination, but his patience was wearing thin. Bash crossed his arms across his chest and spoke through a clenched jaw, "Just tell her what she wants to know."

"I've tried, but she's a disobedient little toy, unwilling to listen and learn," Juno said simply.

Bash's narrowed gaze faltered and turned to me now. I owed Bash so many explanations, but this wasn't the time or place for it. "Tell me about my mother, Juno."

Bash's brown eyes bore into me, and there were so many questions behind them. I had never spoken about my mother, either. I realized there were so many things I refused to share with him. So much of my past I had kept hidden from the man who loved me without a second thought. Guilt. The guilt of it was heavy in my heart. I only hoped I would be given the chance to explain it all to him.

"I met your mother when you were eight years old."

"Are you the reason she left me?"

"I told you; she didn't leave you. If you still refuse to listen, then we are done here."

"I'm sorry…please tell me."

He leaned forward and took a deep breath before continuing.

"I had just turned twenty-one, my pack leader had died, and without a suitable heir, I was next in line to take over as Alpha of Storm Cross Pack. Your mother sought me out. A beautiful, young, gingered child, clinging to her leg."

"I was with her?"

"Yes, Ezra. Your mother didn't leave without you. She wanted safety for herself and her child. She wanted to escape with you."

"Escape what?" Bash asked, fire still burning behind his intense stare.

Juno looked from me to Bash and then laughed. "He doesn't know?"

Bash lunged across the table, his hand clamping around Juno's throat. "Keep laughing, wolf, and I'll rip that insufferable sound right out of you."

"Bash!" I yelled, yanking him back with all my strength. When he crashed back into his chair, I gasped, covering my mouth with my hands. Oh Goddess, what have I just done?

Juno's eyes narrowed into dangerous slits. "You'll regret that, Bash. No one humiliates me and gets away with it."

Bash rose to his feet, his gaze never leaving Juno's. "Bring it on, wolf. I'm not afraid of you."

"Big words when I'm the one chained to this table." Juno snapped back.

I stepped between the two of them, my heart racing. "Enough! Both of you! This isn't solving anything."

The room was thick with tension, everyone watching to see what would happen next. Bash's breathing was heavy, his fists still clenched at his sides. Juno's lips curled into a smirk, but there was a glint of something darker in his eyes. This wasn't over, not by a long shot.

"Bash?" I pleaded. "Please, go."

My words were like daggers, and the look in his eyes was filled with so much hurt that I looked away. When the door slammed behind me, my whole body jolted. I turned to look at Juno. Leaning over the desk until we were just heartbeats apart.

"Tell me what happened next."

I could see the flicker of surprise in Juno's eyes, but he didn't move an inch. My heart raced as I whispered, "What are you hiding, Juno?"

The words hung in the air, heavy with suspicion and anticipation, until he finally sucked in his breath, licked his lips, and then spoke.

"After listening to your mother's story, after hearing of what your father had done to her and to you...I had agreed to allow her to enter my pack."

"He had never hurt me before she left."

"He did. You were so young you had blocked it out, but he did hurt you, Ezra."

"Where is my mother now? What happened? Why didn't we join your pack?"

He sighed, his body language softening once again, "Your father found out. And…"

"What did he do?"

"He killed her."

My arms trembled, threatening to buckle under the weight of his words. I sat back down into the chair, gripping my chest, as I struggled to catch my breath.

"Breathe."

"I don't think I can…my mother was trying to save me, and it cost her…"

"Her life."

"Lana? No more lives will be lost to save me. This ends now."

"Finally. Uncage me. One swipe of my claw, and it will be his end."

"A swift death would be too merciful."

"I always did love a good hunt."

I exited the room to see Bash leaning against the wall.

"Bash," My hand reached for his face, but he caught it at my wrist, stopping me in my tracks. I was afraid now, not of him, but of the very real possibility that I might actually be losing him.

"I've given you every piece of me, everything I have to give, Ezra."

"I know." My voice was barely audible as I continued searching for air where there was none. My lungs were burning with every forced inhale.

"It'll never be enough…will it?"

"You have always been enough, Bash. Please, if I could go back. If I could undo every decision I've ever made…I would. I never meant for any of this to happen."

"And yet it did, and you can't. You asked me to trust you, and you couldn't trust me enough to tell me about your mother…about your dad…any of it."

"It wasn't your pain, Bash. I didn't want you to suffer through it because of me."

"I watched you suffer, Ezra. And I couldn't do anything to stop it because you never let me in. When you hurt, I hurt. Don't you get that?"

"I do now. I didn't then. I didn't know what it felt like to be loved by anyone until you, Bash. Please, I can't lose you; let me explain."

He nuzzled his face into my hand, kissing my fingers, before pulling me into him. "Fuck, I am a fool. I'm hopelessly and helplessly in love with you. I could never leave you, but I can't fight enemies I don't know exist. I need to know everything, Ezra. No more secrets."

"Okay, no more secrets. But first…"

"No more games."

"Good, because I'm not playing any. I've never been more serious about anything in my life. I want you to mark me."

"Ezra?"

"Mark me, Bash. I'm yours. I have always been yours, and I don't care that in two days, the war begins or ends. I want you to…"

Before I could finish my sentence, he was pulling me up into his arms and carrying me outside of the prison.

"Bash?"

"I'm taking you home. You've clearly lost your damn mind."

"I assure you; my mind has never been clearer than it is right now. I want you, and I want you to have all of me."

"Fuck, Ez." He slid me into the passenger seat of the sexiest car I had ever laid eyes on.

"Is this your car?" I asked, looking around as he climbed into the driver's side.

"Yeah, a little too cold for the bike."

"Your car is a 1967 Plymouth GTX? And I've never been in it?"

"You seemed to like the Bike."

"I did; I mean, I do but fuck if this car doesn't make me want you to take me right here and right now."

His eyes darkened, and he burned rubber, leaving the parking lot.

"Bash?"

He shot me a side-eye but didn't say anything as he drove. Focused solely on the road ahead of us.

"Sebastian!" I called out louder.

"Ezra." He didn't look at me, only slammed his foot down on the clutch and shifted into the next gear. The tension building between us was driving me crazy. I could feel the vibrations of the car engine beneath us, matching the quickened pace of my heart.

"What's going on, Bash?" I demanded, trying to steady my voice. He glanced at me briefly before returning his focus to the road, "It's complicated."

"What's complicated? I want you, and you want me…what else is there to complicate?"

"It's not that simple, Ezra," he said, his voice now strained as he shifted gears again, the car accelerating to an unfathomable speed. "I can't risk losing you."

"Why would you lose me? Bash, I love you, and I want this."

Bash's eyes softened for a moment, but his jaw remained tense, "I love you too, Ezra."

"Then why won't you just mark me?"

"Did Zayne put you up to this?"

I didn't answer him. I had talked to Zayne, and yes, it was Zayne's idea…but I wanted this, too. If it would help make him stronger, then I wanted this because I needed him to live. I needed more time to love him.

"Ezra, did Zayne ask you to do this?" His demand that I answer that particular question echoed throughout the car's interior.

"He might have mentioned it, but Bash, I want this."

"Did he tell you that the bond would make us stronger?"

"Yes."

"Did he also tell you that it would connect us in other ways you can't even imagine?"

"I don't see how that could be a bad thing either, Bash."

"You are so strong, Baby girl. But I need you to know all the risks of what you're asking me to do. If I ever mark you, there is no going back. We'll be bound together forever. If one of us dies…"

"What happens if one of us dies?"

His expression grew somber when he answered, "If one of us dies after we're bonded, the other would feel it deeply. Like a part of their soul is missing. The pain would be unbearable, and some say it can even be fatal. It's a risk, Ezra. A testament to how powerful our connection would be. But it isn't a risk I'm willing to wager with your life."

"Pull over."

"Ezra?" His voice trembled as he spoke my name.

"I said pull over, Bash!"

Bash downshifted and then gently pulled the car off to the side of the road. Once he parked, bash took a deep breath, his eyes locking onto mine; he didn't want this because if he died, I could die with him. But there was no version of this life that I would ever want to live without him.

"I need you to live, Ezra. Even if I don't."

"I can't do that! And you can't ask me to. I've made my decision. If I live, it will be because you are here to live this life with me. And if I die, it will be by your side! Fighting for the future of our pack. For our future, us, together. I want all of you for as long as I can have you, Bash. I am yours, and you are mine, so stop deflecting and fucking do it."

No more words were needed. Just two bodies moving together, perfectly in sync, as our intense need for each other reached its peak. He threw his seat back as I kicked my pants down over my ankles, and then he grabbed my hips like he owned me. Pulling me into his lap before lifting my shirt off over my head. Two hearts completely aligned, as I moved my hips so I could unbuckle his jeans, releasing his cock.

His eyes raked up and down my body. "Fuck, Ezra...You're exquisite."

"Shut up and fuck me," I demanded.

He pulled his shirt up over his head, his hair ruffling in the process, before grabbing the straps of my bra, yanking them down over my shoulders, my breasts falling out in front of his face.

"I've waited so long. I think you can wait a few minutes so I can enjoy this."

His mouth moved over my shoulders and down to my breasts, suckling on my nipples as I dipped my hips against his fully erect cock, which brushed against my silk thong near my entrance. I was moaning as I ran my hands through his hair. His tongue swirling over my hard nipples before nipping at them. Whimpers escaped me as his warm tongue and cold breaths sucked my soul right out of my chest. The wetness between my legs, soaking through.

"Bash…" My hands trailed down his body until I held him in my hands. He was so much bigger than I imagined. He made a low, throaty grunt that was almost primal at my touch. His eyes were full-on possessed when he reached down, running his fingers up and down my pussy, over my panties. His lips trailing kisses against my neck.

"Slow down." He whispers in my ear before nibbling on my earlobe, sucking it into his mouth.

"Make me," I breathe through the shivers now running down my body.

He grabs my wrists in one hand and holds them against the roof of the car before sliding my thong to the side. His finger was against my swollen bud, causing me to moan. The smirk on his face told me he knew exactly what he was doing here, but I wanted more of him. No, I needed him.

"Bash? Make me yours?" I begged.

Two can play this game, but I would win. The hunger in his deep raspy groan as he released my hands, gripping my hips and thrusting his cock into my entrance, overpowered my senses. He sounded and felt so damn good. Thrust after thrust, bringing with it more power, more heat, and just before I reached my climax, he gently but firmly sunk his teeth into my shoulder.

At first, the sharp sting felt like fire coursing through my veins until it transformed into a rush of warmth and a sense of belonging. I could feel the connection between us solidifying, binding us together in an unbreakable way. Was I even still breathing? The moan that escaped my lips, as my body quivered in protest of the pure ecstasy radiating from within me, confirmed that I was still, without a doubt, breathing.

And if that wasn't enough confirmation, his hand pulled me down into his kiss before he leaned into me to whisper, "From now on, Ezra, every heartbeat of mine belongs to you."

I was his.

He marked me.

CHAPTER TWENTY-TWO

PROMISE

--Bash's POV

I pushed open the large, oversized wooden doors to my office. The hand-carved doors featured one-of-a-kind brass filigree inlay, different trees, and swirling lines bordering them. The symbol of our Pack. My Pack. The doors were ten feet high, an incredible piece of art, built directly into the foundation of the place where I had grown up, and I don't think I ever took the time to genuinely appreciate them in the 21 years I lived here.

When I walked in, my whole body spun one hundred eighty degrees as I continued to stare in awe at those remarkable wooden doors. I nearly tripped myself in the process, stumbling into the large office. Everything seemed so much more vibrant these last few days since I had marked Ezra. But I quickly recovered from my little stumble in time to see Zayne perched behind my large desk, his feet propped up onto the corner of it.

I walked around the desk, pushing his feet to the ground as I straightened my jacket and leaned back against the desk.

"Zayne, talk to me, buddy. Tell me something I actually want to hear for once."

"Well, someone woke up on the right side of his Luna today."

"No."   My finger was pointing like I was scolding a disobedient little pup. "Just…No, Zayne."

"Okay," he raised his hands palms forward, "moving on. Gabe accepted your challenge, and the elders negotiated the terms based on our pack histories."

"Okay, and what was decided?" I asked, my eyes narrowing as I leaned in closer.

"Well, unfortunately, I won't get to jump in and save your ass. You'll have to win this one on your own." He replied with a smirk playing on his lips as he leaned farther back in my chair, arms crossed.

"When have you ever jumped in to save my ass? You're usually the source of all my problems." I shot back, crossing my arms and raising my eyebrow.

"Name one time." He challenged, tilting his head slightly.

"The boat party?"

"Oh shit, I forgot about that." He muttered, scratching the back of his head.

"Then there was that time freshman year when you welded Professor Marcs' car door shut," I added.

"Oh, come on, that was epic." He said, chuckling.

"And that time down by the river when…" I began, but he cut me off.

"Okay, okay, I got it. There's no need to bring Caydence's naked ass into this. You make a fair point." He conceded, raising his hands up again in mock surrender.

"When does it happen?" I asked as the silence fell around us in waves. Unspoken fear, anxiety, and what-ifs danced about as we exchanged glances. Neither one of us could speak about what might happen if I lost.

"Tomorrow night at dusk, Bash. Alpha to Alpha. The losing pack will either submit or be labeled Rogue. But you have Ezra and the bond now, so you're going to win."

"I could have won without involving her if you had kept your fucking mouth shut!" I snapped back at him. I was still pissed about his meddling. Was being mated with Ezra the best thing that has ever happened to me? Yes, without a doubt. Was her life also in danger now? Yes. I hated myself for succumbing to my own selfish cravings.

"So, suggestion? Why don't we just bottle up all that rage so you can unleash it on Gabe tomorrow night."

"You remember your word, Zayne. If anything happens to me, you make sure she lives through this. I don't care if you have to move heaven and hell to make it happen. You save her."

"I gave you my word. Not as your Beta. Not as your Friend. But as your brother."

We might have shared a hug then, but Ezra came storming into the room. A cute little cinder burning as bright as her red locks. I cleared my throat and met her around the desk.

"Ah, my Luna. You look ravishing, like a fire lily in full bloom. Your beauty ignites a flame within me that no storm could ever extinguish."

"Oh, don't you fucking start; you cannot just sweet talk your way out of this!"

"I'm not trying to. I just wanted you to know what the sight of you does to me."

"…and that's my cue to get the fuck out of here." Zayne flashed Ezra a smile, which she returned before the blazing anger behind those baby-blue eyes turned back on me with all its fury.

"I'm guessing kisses aren't going to fix this?" I asked, pulling her close to me.

"You left me, Bash. All by myself. I woke up, and you were gone!" she pouted, looking up at me.

"I'm sorry, Ez. I should've been more considerate of your feelings. I didn't want to wake you," I said as I brushed my thumb over her bottom lip. She sucked it into her mouth, biting down on it. Everything she did, and everything she was, was so addictive.

As I cradled her face, my other hand resting on the small of her back, I leaned down and drew her bottom lip into my mouth. She gasped, and her hands wrapped around my neck as she rose to her tiptoes; I scooped her up, and her legs wrapped around my waste. As I moved us around the desk and laid her in the desk chair, my tongue slid between her lips and swirled around her tongue. She reacted with faint moans of pleasure, and I couldn't keep my hands from exploring her body.

I could feel her lust for me, which just caused my growing hunger for her to swell. A low, guttural grunt, a sound filled with raw emotion and unspoken promises, escaped me as my hand slid up her outer thigh.

She pulled away from me, our eyes locking momentarily.

"Bash?" she whispered as I lowered myself to my knees before her.

"Wearing your elegant little outfits will not stop my primal behavior, Ez. Now lift your hips for me so I can rip these pantyhose off and eat that delicious, sweet hole like a fucking animal."

Her breathing hitched as she complied with my demand, holding onto the chair to help counter her weight as my hands dug into the top of her pantyhose, ripping them down over her beautiful curvy ass.

"Such a good girl. Now…" I pressed firmly against her inner thighs, "Open."

"Oh Goddess," she moaned as she spread her thighs for me.

Every sweet whimper, every shudder of her body, as I kissed up her thighs, left her pussy glistening. She looked delicious, and I could feel my cock twitching upright as my tongue moved in hungry swirls against her little pink starburst. I placed two fingers inside, curving and flicking inside her until my fingers were imbued with every angelic quality of her pussy.

Her thighs squeezing my head as she orgasmed against my tongue was earth-shattering. Her hands were ruffling through my hair as I slid my tongue inside her, and her body trembled in ecstasy.

"Please, Bash, I need you." She whispered as she tried to push my face away. But I hadn't had enough. I flicked my tongue against her clit, each flick…another gasp, another tremble. Fuck me, she was perfect.

"Tell me what you want, Baby girl," I said as I stood up and released the clasp on my belt. The look in her eyes was hypnotic.

"I want you. Please, I need to feel you." She cried out.

"Mm. Fuck, Baby girl." I picked her up and laid her across the desk, pulling her to the edge, then inserted myself while I pushed her legs up to her chest so I could hit her deeper. As I thrust into her, she screamed, "Harder." Which I was happy to oblige. Somewhere in the mix of thrusting and grunting and her sexy moans, things may or may not have gone tumbling off the desk. Her sudden laughs had her pussy tightening around my cock, "Eyes on me," I said as she scanned the room to see what we broke.

"I'm about to cum, Babygirl," I said as her eyes met mine, and as I went to pull out, she moaned, "No, don't."

"Ezra?" I said, pained and about to bust.

"I want to feel you fill me up," she said.

One more thrust was all it took. Her pussy was clutching onto me so hard as I felt my release. I leaned forward, kissing her neck as she clung to me.

When she whispered, "You're forgiven." I managed a chuckle of my own.

"Oh, is that all it takes?"

"Mhmm." Her lips curved softly, a sweet flirtation that made my heart race.

"I love you, Ez."

"I love you too," she said, looking around at the mess of broken glass and scattered paperwork. "We broke your desk lamp."

"I hated that lamp anyway." I said as I kissed her forehead, "And it was worth it."

"Bash?" Her smile was replaced with a wistful look that warned of both longing and sadness.

I moved a stray hair back behind her ear, and her eyes closed as she melted into my touch.

"What's wrong, Baby girl?"

She pulled me into her hug, her head nuzzled into my chest. "It's not too late. You don't need to do this. We could find another way…"

"Ezra. If I could disappear into this moment with you, I would. From the moment I met you, my world shifted. Every day since I've found myself falling deeper and deeper in love with you. Your smile, your laughter, your kindness, they light up my life in ways I never thought possible.

I've never felt this way before, and I'm scared, too. It's like you unlocked a part of my heart I didn't even know existed. You make me want to be a better man, to strive for more, to dream bigger. But" my pain was palpable, radiating from my very being as I wrapped her into my arms, "Gabe's pack is growing in strength and power. This moment was inevitable the second he put his hands on you. I won't stop until he's gone and you're safe. You complete me, Ezra. You are everything: my heart, my soul. I love you with every fiber of my being, and this isn't the end for us. I promise I will stand by your side, forever and always, my little Luna."

"That isn't a promise you can make."

"Yes, I can because I know you make me stronger, Ez. I also know there is no force in this world that is strong enough to take you from me. Especially not Gabriel Knight."

"Bash. You've shown me a love that I never knew existed, and I can't imagine my life without you, either. The thought of you battling Gabriel? It terrifies me, not because I don't think you're strong enough or brave enough, I know that you are. I just...we haven't had enough time. I need you to come back to me. You're my heart, my soul, and I'll hold onto the hope that we'll have our forever together."

"Don't be sad, Baby girl. We will have our forever. I'm far from done loving you."

CHAPTER TWENTY-THREE

I SWEAR IT ON THE GODDESS

--Ezra's POV

The sky tonight was deep, inky black. The air was polluted with so much unrest that it felt thick, almost suffocating, as if the world itself were holding its breath. The only sliver of light from the silver moon above that pierced through the thick clouds that hung over Oakland. Even the Goddess seemed to retreat tonight, a sign of her disapproval.

Every sound seemed amplified: the rustling of the leaves as they were swept away in the breeze, the distant howls of wolves as they approached the college, and the soft murmur of our Gammas and Elders as they took their places in the large Courtyard within the College.

The chill of the night air seeped into my bones, making the hairs on the back of my neck stand on end. My heart was pounding with such ferocity in my chest, a sense of impending doom hastening my pulse with every passing second. Every breath felt forced, like I was the one fighting for my survival.

Bash looked at me, pleading one last time, "You don't need to watch this. Let Kit take you home."

I looked from Bash to Kit, who stood at my side. She grabbed my hand, reassuring me that she supported my decision, no matter what.

"I am your Luna, Bash. And I'll remain at your side." I said with finality. This was a debate we have had several times over the last day, but I refused to hide from the spotlight. I would be here to support my Alpha, my mate. Nothing he could say was going to change my mind.

"Tonight, I fight for our pack, our pride, and our survival. But I will hold you again, Ezra. I swear it on the Goddess, the silver moon, our witness."

Before I could reply, Gabriel approached with a menacing aura, his eyes glowing with an unnatural light. His anger was palpable, and it seemed to manifest through contorting features as if the beast within him was clawing to break free.

"Well, well, Bash," he sneered, his voice dripping with malice. "Looks like you've got yourself quite a little love story here. How touching."

Bash stood his ground, his fists clenched and his heart pounding. I wondered if he could feel my fear as I stood beside him. If he did, it only served to fuel his determination, as he didn't show it. Gabriel's gaze shifted hungrily to me, a predatory smile curling on his lips. I couldn't believe I had ever let that beast touch me. What was I thinking? How did I not see his true nature?

"Don't worry, Kitten," Gabriel taunted, his voice a dangerous whisper. "When this is all over, you'll be mine again. I'll make sure of it."

Bash's protectiveness and primal instincts seemed to roar to life as he stepped forward, placing himself between me and Gabe, his own wolf, Dane, coming forward. This was so much more than a battle between Alpha's. This was a fight for me, for our love, for his survival, and for everything that mattered.

"I'm going to enjoy this," Gabe said before turning and walking to the center of the arena. He grabbed two swords and took a fighting stance. He looked deadly, and I reached up, cupping Bash's face with trembling hands. I kissed him with all the love, and passion I felt for this man, who I was unmistakenly in love with. Everything around us faded away until it was just his lips against mine, a brief sanctuary before the storm. As we pulled apart, he rested his forehead against mine. We shared one final breath before he turned and walked to the middle of the arena.

Before Bash had even grabbed his weapons, Gabe lunged at him, his movements quick and feral. Bash had managed to dodge the first blows; his instincts were sharp. As he countered with a powerful strike, my heart beamed with pride. The two grappled fiercely, each blow echoing, followed by the howling and chanting of their packs as they continued to strike, parry, and counter the other's attacks.

I watched them, unable to tear my eyes away, torn between my fear and his determination. I knew the outcome of this fight would shape our future, and I had let my guard down in the heat of the battle.

"EZRA, RUN!" Kit yelled, but it was too late. Gabe's beta, Thomas, lunged at me, wrapping his arms around me and holding me tightly, knocking Kit to the side. The impact left her body unmoving. I screamed out, trying to break free of his grasp. He could easily crush me.

I watched Bash's focus waver for a moment, his eyes watching me with horror. That was all Gabe needed. He took advantage of the distraction, landing a vicious blow that sent Bash staggering backward. Gabe's grin was feral, sensing his victory.

Thomas tightened his grip around me. This was it. I was going to die.

"THOMAS!" Zayne yelled as he burst through the crowd around us with fierce determination in his eyes. With a swift, calculated maneuver, he took down Thomas, freeing me from his clutches. As I got to my feet, I heard Gabe taunting Bash.

"Looks like you're not as strong as you thought," his voice was dripping in triumph as Bash struggled to regain his footing. He could feel everything I felt, and it was clear he was having trouble focusing. Oh Goddess, I was going to be the reason he lost. The bond was going to kill him.

I pushed through the crowd of wolves and stepped into the arena. I watched Gabe land a fatal blow, his sword gleaming wickedly in the dim light as it struck Bash. My cries pierced the air, desperation fueling every step as I closed the distance between us. I reached him just as his strength began to wane. Our eyes met one last time.

"Bash!" I cried out with urgency and love, but the gravity of the situation echoed in the paling hue of his eyes. "No, no, no, no," I cried as I pressed my hands against his bloody chest, trying to stop the bleeding, but there was so much blood. How could there be this much blood?

"You're gonna be okay; you promised you'd be okay; you can't leave me; just hold on, please…"

"I'm sorry," his voice was so weak, "Ezra…I love you," he whispered as he took his last breath. His eyes rolled back into his head as his body grew limp beneath my touch.

The pain in my chest was the most excruciating pain I'd ever felt like my heart was being ripped out of my chest. I collapsed over the bloody shell of the man I loved, writhing in agony as the bond severed. The howl that escaped me was a raw, visceral reaction that echoed through the night. Lana was disoriented and heartbroken. Nothing was right.

I was shocked. Devastated by the loss of my mate. I could barely process what was happening around me. As I felt hands gripping me, Lana resisted fiercely. I was being pulled backward, and I was fighting with any strength I had left to move forward, back to Bash. I needed to be closer to Bash.

Suddenly, Zayne lunged at Gabe, their clash a whirlwind of fury and desperation. "I've got you, Ezra!" he shouted, his voice cutting through the chaos.

Zayne fought with everything he had. His moves were precise and powerful. Gabe's grip on me loosened as Zayne's relentless attacks forced him to retreat. With one final, decisive blow, Zayne sent Gabe staggering back.

Zayne turned to me, his expression softening as he saw my pain. "Come on, Ezra," he urged gently, taking my hand and pulling me to my feet. "We need to get out of here."

I just stood there, staring at Bash's lifeless body.

"He wouldn't want you to die here, Ezra. Now move your ass!" he yelled as he pulled me after him. The chaos around us, finally coming into focus. So much for ending the war before it began. This was a fucking bloodbath. And we were directly in the center of it.

As we ran, I picked up speed. I glanced back one last time at Bash, my heart aching with every step. Zayne's grip was firm, his presence a steady anchor in the storm of my grief. He had kept his promise to Bash, and now he was my lifeline.

"Where's Kit?"

He didn't reply; just kept pulling me forward.

"Zayne! Where's Kit?!?!" I screamed, planting my feet firmly into the ground; I wasn't leaving without her.

"I had Gamma Dalton take her to the pack house now if you want to live to see her..." He ducked and kicked a wolf hard in the chest, knocking him to the ground, "Run!"